The short stories in this colle  entries in the 2009 FLOW competition.

FLOW (the Forces Literary Organisation Worldwide) for All is dedicated to offering assistance to those who have suffered from the effects of war, especially the suffering shared by servicemen and women, their relatives and their friends.

Proceeds from the sale of this book will be used to support the work of FLOW for All, helping them to become a registered charity and to employ counsellors for those in need of care and support.

For more information please visit the following websites:
flowforall.org
flowsforum.com
forcespoetry.com
forcesstories.com

Stories of the Poppies

Short Story Collection – Volume 1

FLOW for All patron Dame Vera Lynn DBE
(Image © Giles Penfound)

Published in paperback by Silverwood Books 2009

www.silverwoodbooks.co.uk

Copyright © FLOW for All 2009

The right of FLOW for All to be identified as the authors of this work
has been asserted by them in accordance with the Copyright,
Designs and Patents Act 1988.

ISBN 978-1-906236-26-7

British Library Cataloguing in Publication Data
A CIP catalogue record for this book is available from the British Library

Set in 11pt Bembo by SilverWood Books

STORIES OF THE POPPIES

SHORT STORY COLLECTION – VOLUME 1

from

FLOW for All

The Forces Literary Organisation Worldwide

SilverWood

Also available from www.silverwoodbooks.co.uk

Voices of the Poppies Poetry Anthology
(introduced by Dame Vera Lynn)

Poems of the Poppies Poetry Anthology Volume 1

Please exercise caution
as some of the stories in this collection may be
considered unsuitable for younger readers.

INTRODUCTION

Mac Macdonald – co-founder FLOW for All

Welcome to the first short story collection from The Forces Literary Organisation Worldwide for All (FLOW for All).

Our initial organisation, Forces Poetry, was set up in 2005. As we grew we attracted not just poems but stories as well and so Forces Stories was born and FLOW for All was created to become the front of house organisation.

Our aim is to support those who suffer from the effects of war, and to offer a place online where anyone could come to freely express their emotions. Little did we know that within four years we'd be running competitions and publishing volumes of poetry and short stories!

Our first competitions were opened in April 2009 and ran for four months. Two competitions ran alongside each other – one accepting submissions of poetry, the other short stories. We received a consistently high standard of entries covering a range of subjects, and all entries were posted on either Forces Poetry or Forces Stories. There were no official judges; stories and poems were selected for the published collection in the most democratic way – by encouraging all visitors to vote for their favourite story or poem. The top twenty stories made it into *Stories of the Poppies* and the top seventy poems are to be published in *Poems of the Poppies*.

Reading the entries, visitors to the forums met a wonderful cast of characters and nationalities, spent time in a variety of locations and eras, and experienced an array of emotions. Some stories were uplifting, some touched on conflict and war, others reflected on loss and human dignity. Authors had written from their hearts, and this gave them the ability to reach out and touch the hearts of others.

FLOW for All would like to thank everyone who submitted their work to this year's competition and everyone who voted. Special mention should go to the moderators of flowsforums.com, who helped everything run so smoothly in spite of the occasional technical hiccup – thank you for your dedication and for giving so freely of your time.

And finally, congratulations to the twenty authors whose work makes up this year's wonderful collection.

Thank you for purchasing this book and therefore helping us to "light up the darkness".

Mac Macdonald
2009

Contents

FOREWORD

Major-General Tim Cross CBE

The stories contained in this little book sit within the best
traditions of war poetry and writing. Challenging and moving
in equal measure they provide a window into the individual
hearts and minds of just some of those who are living with the
consequences of having been caught up in the sorts of wars and
battles that many believed we would never be involved in again.

The vast majority of the soldiers that I commanded over the
years were not just good people – they and their families were
quite simply some of the most impressive people I ever met.
From fighting their way into places like Iraq and Afghanistan,
to patrolling the streets on counter-insurgency operations
around the world, they responded with humanity and humour
to whatever faced them. And far from being unthinking
automatons, keen for a fight and uncaring of the consequences,
they asked serious questions and felt deeply about what they
were engaged in.

For many of them, the military is the one place where
they find true friendship. But along with the memories of the
good times, when they individually and collectively made a
tremendous difference to the lives of those caught up in the
maelstrom of war, they carry too the memories of the violence
and the failures – and, in particular, the memories of the death
and injury of those friends.

For some – indeed many – the experiences build and
enhance their confidence. But many struggle to come to terms
with all that they have seen and heard – and some are locked in
depression and loneliness. Abandoned by those that sent them off
to war, all too often they and their families are left alone to face
up to the events that they have been through, in a world that has
little or no comprehension of what they have experienced.

Being able to talk and write about what they have
experienced is a part of the healing process. So, read what they
have to say with pride – and as you do, please build inside

yourself a resolve not to forget this new generation of soldiers and their loved ones who have been, and continue to be, at the front line of dealing with humanity's failings.

Major-General Tim Cross CBE
2009

FOREWORD

Ruth Rayment

On the 4th August 2004 my nuclear family changed forever. The idea of what a family should be – a mum, dad, sister and brother – was abruptly ended and I have no doubt it is a day I shall never forget.

My brother, Pte Christopher Gordon Rayment, died through an accidental death in Iraq, Al Amarah at 11.30am. By 5.30pm that day we had two people from Woolwich, Royal Artillery Barracks inform my family of Christopher's death. It was almost like the clock had stopped for us; my family had suddenly become a statistic, my brother another name on the list of many who had already died in the name of terrorism.

After Christopher died, as his youngest sister I struggled to deal with his death, as did many people in my family. This was my first death, and the whole process of grief was completely overwhelming beyond all words. I went through every stage of grief imaginable and at one point I wondered if I were ever going to feel the same again. The only way I can describe it is being stuck down a huge hole and not being able to climb to the top to get out.

Then just when I feared there would never be an answer or resolve to my emotions and the way I was feeling, I discovered the Forces Poetry website, which is part of The Forces Literary Organisation Worldwide (FLOW for All). I began writing poetry, something I had a passion for at the age of thirteen. Now at sixteen years of age I found my only comfort in my brother's death was writing about him or my new found faith, which also gave me the inner strength to pull through a traumatic event in my life.

When I'm writing poetry, even to this day, five years on from Christopher's death, I feel like I'm in a whole new world, a different element, and everything that is within my mind pours out and is formed into yet another poem. When I'm writing I think about the pain, the loss, the anger and the torment my mind went through, and then I return back to reality and see what these emotions have enabled me to create.

I sincerely hope this short story collection *Stories of the Poppies* will help FLOW for All achieve their admirable aim of being able to offer assistance to anyone who has been affected by war and conflict.

Ruth Rayment
2009

Stories of the Poppies

Short Story Collection – Volume 1

Heroes, Every One

Roland Gardner

When I was a lad, (how often have we heard that phrase from our elders and betters), my heroes were not those of my peers.

My mates spoke in hushed tones of Tommy Lawton, Nat Lofthouse, Johnny Haynes and, of course, the incomparable Stan Matthews. Not that I disliked sport you understand. I was watching our little nine inch television one magical Saturday afternoon when an eighteen year old Fred Trueman tore the Indian touring side to shreds in a devastating opening spell. I've been an avid follower of cricket ever since.

No. I'm talking about real heroes. Where my friends had pictures of the great footballers on their bedroom walls – I had my collection of shrapnel in a drawer. Cannon shell cases from German aircraft, a twisted shred of doodlebug fuselage, misshapen fragments of anti aircraft shell, and best of all a few precious spent 303 bullets from a Spitfire or Hurricane.

My heroes were Johnny Johnson, Bob Doe, Robert Stanford-Tuck, Roland Beaumont and Cats Eyes Cunningham.

The last was a famous night fighter ace – scourge of German bomber crews marauding over our beloved England under cover of darkness. My Mum used to tell me that Cats Eyes owed his extraordinary night vision to the carrots that he ate by the handful. Wishing to be like him I, of course, ate my carrots. In my imagination Cats Eyes spurned a radio operator. On the seat beside him sat a bag of carrots - whenever he felt that his magical eyesight was losing its edge he would dip into it.

My heroes were, without exception, modest men. When questioned about their heroic deeds, they would tend to look downwards and claim that anyone in their position would have done the same.

By the age of three and a bit, I had studied the aircraft identification chart which was published periodically by all good newspapers (the *Daily Mirror*). Therefore, I could tell a 109 from a Spitfire and a Focke Wulf 190 from a Tempest. Not only, might I add, by their appearance, but also from the sound of their engines.

I had seen a doodlebug pursued by a Spitfire (which I think was losing the race) and I had heard the loudest silence in the world when the motor of another one stopped. At that point I was snatched up by my mother and unceremoniously bundled under the kitchen table until we heard a dull crump some distance away.

No, I didn't want to score a hat trick in the cup final, I wanted to fly a Spitfire.

Of course, by the time that I was old enough to join the RAF not only was the Spitfire long retired, but by economic necessity I had to go and work in the real world. But my fascination with those glorious pilots and my reverence for their exploits never diminished.

When my heroic career dreams had long been laid to rest, in the last few years leading up to retirement I worked behind the bar in a local pub. There I met a man in his early seventies who had achieved my boyhood ambition of joining the RAF. His name was Alan and he was what our American cousins would have called 'a line-shooter.'

Like me, he had grown up to hero worship the wartime RAF pilots and, almost inevitably, wanted to be a Spitfire pilot. Unlike me, his parents could afford to keep him at school long enough to gain the qualifications necessary to secure him a place in the RAF. Of course, by the time that he was old enough to become a pilot, the magnificent Spitfires were long gone, and he flew a Lightning Fighter.

Maybe.

According to him, he had trained initially as a rear gunner in a Lancaster bomber, and switched to fighters at a later date.

I knew that this was most unlikely to be true. For one thing, I had seen the rear gun turret of a Lancaster, and Alan was about fifty percent too large to fit into it. Secondly, one did not skate between Bomber and Fighter Command. Once you were in bombers, there you stayed.

I didn't really mind him fantasising about various aspects of his service life. I just thought it a bit sad that he felt the need – that was all. To be absolutely honest, I didn't like him that much.

One lunch time when the rush was over, Alan told me this story.

When he was ten years old he went to Maidstone Grammar School. The following year was 1940, that magnificent summer when the young lads of RAF Fighter Command fought the Luftwaffe to a standstill over the green fields of Kent. That series of engagements, the most glorious page in our decidedly spotty history, afterwards became known as the Battle of Britain.

The school in those days was set on the edge of the town in fields bordering Mote Park. One afternoon, shortly after the autumn term started, young Alan and his friend were far more interested in craning their necks to watch the activity in the sky than in paying attention to their lessons. Indeed, who wouldn't have been?

Anyway, just before afternoon break they spotted a Hurricane fighter circling the fields a couple of hundred yards from the school.

As soon as they could escape, they hopped over the school boundary, and sprinted in the direction that they had seen the plane. To their unbounded joy, they discovered that the fighter had landed in a field and the pilot had taxied his aircraft under the overhanging branches of a nearby oak tree. When the boys arrived he was leaning against the tail of his Hurricane, smoking a cigarette, whilst keeping an eye on the aerial activity.

Grinning at his adoring audience, he explained that he had been forced to drop out of the battle going on above because his engine was overheating. The lads helpfully pointed out that Detling airfield was only about a mile away to the west and West Malling a couple of miles in the other direction. He said that the ground crews were far too busy for him to bother them, and about twenty minutes would be sufficient for his motor to cool down.

Having stubbed out his second cigarette, he clambered into his cockpit and started the Merlin engine. Taxiing round to face down the length of the field he opened up the motor and took off. The two boys, who had completely lost sight of the fact that their break was long over, waved frantically as he climbed away.

The pilot waggled his wings briefly at the watching boys and flew off.

As you can imagine, Alan and his friend were full of the close encounter with their heroic fighter pilot.

These were exciting times and between lessons in the air raid shelters, the boys were watching history being made before their very eyes.

Two days later, they could hardly believe their luck when a Hurricane started circling the same spot, this time just before school finished for the day. The lads hurtled over to the field and there was their pilot, smoking his cigarette and grinning at them. They were so glad to see him that they forgot to ask him why he was back again.

The twosome plied him with questions about how many 109s he had shot down and what it was like to see 'the whites of the Hun's eyes.'

This time he stayed long enough to smoke three cigarettes, lighting each one from the stub of the last. Alan's friend afterwards recalled that he had difficulty in lighting them, because his hands were shaking. Before he left Alan made the observation that the fighter's gun ports were still covered by tape.

"I've had no luck yet today," confided their friend.

After he took off and retracted his wheels, the boys' excitement was complete when the pilot fired a short burst on his guns before disappearing. They never saw him again.

I was completely captivated by this little snapshot of life in a period of history which had fascinated me for as long as I could remember. None-the-less, there were a couple of questions burning a hole in my mind that simply wouldn't let me alone.

The next time that Alan came into the pub, I took him back to our conversation about 'his' fighter pilot.

"Assuming that his story of the overheating engine was true, as it just might have been, why didn't he land at one of the nearby airfields, where they could probably have given him a replacement aircraft?" I asked.

Alan stayed quiet.

"And why did he land at the same place again? In all my

readings of contemporary literature, the Merlin was not prone to overheating.

And why did he fire his guns when he took off the second time?

Could it have been so that he could report that he had been in combat?"

Alan looked at me for what seemed like a long time.

"They were all heroes you know – every one of them."

At that moment I almost liked him.

Felix

Helen Tirebuck

"I would like to introduce you to my son Felix," translated Sergio, my travel companion and interpreter from the local dialect to English. He was speaking on behalf of the youngish looking father who had just introduced himself as George.

Standing in a remote village at the furthest western point in Mozambique before the land becomes Zimbabwe; George has approached us tentatively at first. His right hand extended for a handshake, laying his left hand on the wrist of his outstretched arm as Mozambican custom dictates.

I responded in my best Portuguese that I would very much like to meet Felix prompting George to spin on his heels and lead the way towards his mud hut on the opposite side of the makeshift village football pitch to where we had been speaking.

Advancing across the hard baked ground cracked into a mud mosaic by the intense heat from the African sun overhead, a bunch of children intently watched us approach. Once we passed the point considered by the youngest children as their safe distance from these approaching strangers, they frantically dispersed leaving only the older, bolder kids solemnly clustered together.

George gestured to one of the children and the group parted to allow one child to move to the front of the cluster. I immediately recognized this boy as Felix.

Felix is nine years old; the children he stands amongst are his school friends. Every day they leave their family's huts, joining one another along the way as they travel along the well worn track from their village to the next to attend school. After school they retrace their steps playing their childhood games on the way until they safely reach home.

Each child has been sternly warned not to stray from the path. Each child knows they shouldn't wander into the bush. But they are children and children do as children do.

As Felix slowly moved towards our group the sad reality of my ability to recognize this young boy I had never met before was solely because he moved with the aid of makeshift crutches. Felix has only one leg.

When Felix was eight years old he innocently crossed a patch of shrubland close to his village. Tragically the land was peppered with landmines, a remnant of the long war fought well before Felix had even been born. He ran across one of the mines initiating it to explode right beneath him. Felix miraculously survived this horrific accident which has left him an amputee for the rest of his life. Now when he walks to school he does so with the aid of his crutches. He can't run like all his friends and working as a farmer or cow herder like his elders will be hard if not impossible for this young boy.

Mozambique is a country slowly recovering after suffering twenty years of brutal fighting. Sadly for Felix, his village is one of many in Mozambique where the aftermath of the war continues to resonate for its inhabitants.

In my job of mine clearance I hear stories like Felix's all too often. Laying a landmine costs a dollar or so. Safely finding, clearing and destroying that landmine costs more than 100 times that and is a slow, arduous, painstaking process.

Landmines are indiscriminate and that's the problem. Although laid during times of conflict, these powerful and destructive items of war can quietly lie for decades just a few inches under the ground until somebody sets the pressure of a footstep onto it. That somebody can as readily be a child playing a game of football with their friends as a soldier on patrol.

The 1997 Ottawa Mine Ban Treaty, banning the use of landmines, has brought some constructive hope for the future but until the ban is signed and ratified on a global scale, the threat of yet another young life being permanently shattered remains. By 2009 most countries have signed although amazingly more than thirty have not –including the USA, Russia and China.

So what is the justification to continue in the use of landmines during conflict thus forcing communities like Felix's to live their lives post-conflict in the middle of a minefield?

As Felix stood there perching on his tiny wooden crutches I failed to identify a single compelling argument.

THE PRINGLE SISTERS

Oliver Eade

Violet was sitting at the kitchen table, totally absorbed in her book. Before her, on the table, was a cold cup of tea and a half-eaten biscuit. Her sister, Daphne, called out from her arm-chair throne in the sitting room:

"Violet, are you going to just sit around all day, or are you going to at least think about getting my lunch? All my life I've slaved away for both of us, and here I am, at my age, having to beg for a little help from my younger sister!"

For a while Violet continued to read against the verbal tirade from the sitting room. Then, without looking up, she folded the corner of the page, closed her book, and went quietly over to the cupboard. The telephone in the kitchen rang just as she opened the cupboard door. She picked it up and put it to her ear.

At eighty-eight Daphne, the elder sister, still had a mind that was razor sharp, and she kept as close an eye upon her sister's movements about the house as she had always done. All day long she fired barbed questions at the younger woman who now rarely replied, for an invisible wall had gradually developed between them. At first, after their mother had died and Violet was compelled to live with Daphne, she'd found it difficult to put up with her elder sister's persistent nagging. She would stand up for herself and answer back. Slowly, painfully, she discovered that this approach was pointless. It only resulted in an intensified verbal attack from Daphne. Violet began to learn that if she were to remain quietly submissive then her sister's anger would transform into a constant muttering about all the burdens and responsibilities that she, Daphne, had to bear.

Violet loved books. She'd abandoned the idea of teaching early on when she was offered the position of assistant librarian at the local public library. Displaying no ambition to further her career, she remained in the same poorly-paid post until she retired at sixty. Like her mother, she was one of life's dreamers, and could not have been more different from her elder sister.

Daphne resembled her father in appearance and in character. Major Pringle had been killed in action early on during the second world war. He'd doted upon Daphne, but was forever criticising and castigating the younger of the two girls. Violet would cling to her mother whenever their father was at home, carefully watching his every movement with her large, sad brown eyes. Even this seemed to irritate the man. Daphne was only too eager to team up with her father against her little sister whenever the opportunity arose. As a consequence, the bond between Violet and her mother became very strong. They understood each other perfectly. When the twelve year-old Violet got news of her father's death she skipped around the house happily waving the telegram. She received no reprimand from Mrs Pringle who knew precisely how her daughter felt. By then Daphne had already left home to take up a junior placement with the Ministry of Defence.

Unlike Violet, Daphne had ambition. Lots of it. She soon climbed the career ladder in the Civil Service, and ended up with a very senior position in the War Ministry. She proudly reminded Violet on countless occasions how secret her job was, not that Violet really had the remotest interest in what her elder sister got up to at work. Daphne's retirement pension well exceeded Violet's salary when the latter was still in employment, and Violet's own final pension was meagre indeed. The house, together with all other assets, had been left to Daphne in her father's will. There was nothing that Mrs Pringle could have done to change this, and Violet remained forever dependent on her sister.

It was a great comfort to Violet's mother to have the younger girl at home with her during her last few years of life. When Violet was still only sixteen, she studied for entry into a teacher training college. Violet was a lovely girl, and Mrs Pringle was always on the lookout for a young man who might propose to her someday. She never told Daphne about allowing Violet to go to the RAF dances with her friends. She knew that Violet's censorious sister, who only returned home once every month or two, would never have approved.

At one stage Violet thought that she would never get over the death, from tuberculosis, of her mother, but she did. In fact, somehow she became stronger. She learned how to deal with her sister's moods and tempers herself. Of course, her own circumstances prevented her from becoming independent of her sister, and Daphne took much pleasure in constantly reminding Violet of this. Daphne had moved back to the family home after Mrs Pringle died, and commuted daily by train to London.

No one ever expected Daphne to marry. Her unappealing looks aside, she had a self-centred nature that prevented any close relationship with the opposite sex, regardless of which she'd never really had time for any man other than her own father. It was accepted that for Daphne a proposal of marriage was simply out of the question. Violet's apparent celibacy, however, was a different matter altogether. Although her beauty faded somewhat over the years, she remained a most becoming and pleasant woman. It was certainly a great mystery to most acquaintances of the Pringles as to why the younger of the two sisters had never married. After all, many men would have found her attractive figure and her gentle, albeit dreamy, personality most endearing. Some blamed Violet's failure to free herself from Daphne on this dreaminess. Much of the time Violet seemed to be in her own little world, and perhaps would-be suitors might have found it difficult to break through her defensive shell, although, in truth, the shell was thinner than it appeared to be. Nevertheless, most folk blamed Daphne for blocking Violet's chances of marriage, and amongst themselves they agreed that Daphne's jealousy of Violet's good looks was at the root of the problem.

For whatever the reason, the two sisters stayed together as the years rolled by. Lifelong spinsterhood was clearly their destiny, and other people forgot Daphne and Violet's differences. The two ladies simply became known as 'the Pringle sisters', as though they were one.

Violet went as white as a sheet as she stood in the kitchen clutching the phone to her ear.

"Who is it?" Daphne called out.

Violet's hand holding the phone trembled. She pulled up a chair and sat down as she listened to the voice at the other end of the line.

"Violet! Who is it?" Daphne shouted.

Finally Violet, who'd only spoken a few faltering words into the telephone, put down the handset.

"For me, Daphne!"

"Who?"

"Daphne, it was for me."

"Well don't forget who has to pay for the phone bill!"

"They phoned me, Daphne. Don't worry yourself."

Violet had to concentrate hard as she prepared lunch for her sister, for her thoughts were far away. Even Daphne noticed her curious excitement.

"Why are you grinning, Violet?"

Every morning Violet became excited when the post arrived, and she would hurry to the door.

"What's the rush for?" Daphne would ask. "The postman's not going to take it away again once he's put it through the letter box."

Then one morning a particularly large envelope hit the doormat with a muffled thud. Violet knew this was it. It had a blue airmail label on it. She looked at the unfamiliar stamp. On it was written 'U.S Post'. Her fingers shook with excitement as she held the envelope, turning it over to see the sender's hand-written address, then back again to look at the stamp once more. She took the envelope into the privacy of the kitchen, where she knew she'd be completely safe from Daphne's hawk-like eyes, despite the fact that Daphne was still in bed upstairs having one of her off days.

Violet opened the envelope very carefully with a knife. She shook out its contents onto the kitchen table. She read the letter, all three pages of it, several times. Staring at the hand-writing, with tears in her eyes, she gently stroked the dried ink script with the tips of her fingers, as though this would bring her closer to the writer. Violet picked up the writer's photograph that had fallen out of the envelope with the letter.

"So like Alan," she muttered, tears trickling down her cheeks. "So like him," she repeated, touching the photograph.

Violet returned the letter and its other contents to the envelope. She placed this in the book she was reading. Daphne never touched Violet's books. She hated books.

I'll wait until the last possible moment before telling her, thought Violet, as she set about the day's chores.

Violet had six weeks to sort out her affairs. She would have to renew her passport. Their last trip abroad had been almost twenty years before – a visit to Tuscany which proved to be a disaster. Ten days of nagging from Daphne, Violet ran out of books to read and to complete the picture Daphne fell ill with diarrhoea. This, it turned out, was Violet's fault for insisting they ate at a romantic little restaurant in a hill-top village near Bagni di Lucca. Violet had earfuls about this for some years to come, and they never went abroad together again.

There was also the question of money. Violet had a little in her bank account. This she withdrew and converted to US dollars. However, he did say, in a later telephone call, that she really wouldn't need to bring any money at all. She would be met at the airport in Boston, and he had arranged for a friend of his in London to take her to Heathrow early on the morning of the flight. As the day approached she felt more and more excited, and nothing that Daphne said seemed to irritate her any longer. She would just smile back at her grumpy sister and say, "Yes, Daphne," or "No, Daphne." Of course, she'd done her best to make arrangements to ensure her sister would be cared for. Mrs Williams would drop in daily, clean the house twice a week and do the laundry. Groceries would continue to be delivered to the door and, whether she liked it or not, Daphne Pringle would be getting meals on wheels every day. She could then direct complaints about her food to the council rather than to Violet. Most of all, Daphne could be reassured that would no longer have the financial burden of her younger sister. Surely she would be pleased about this?

Violet had set her alarm clock for six in the morning on the day of her departure. The pick-up for the airport was to be at seven o'clock. Daphne never got up before eight-thirty, so Violet came into her sister's bedroom the evening before, just before Daphne would normally turn out her light.

"Violet, you really should knock before coming into my room, you know."

It had been another of her off days.

"Don't worry, sister. I won't do that again. In fact, after tomorrow I shall never be seeing you again. You see, I'm flying to Boston tomorrow to stay with my son. He invited me over at first, and sent me the air tickets, but the last time he spoke with me he said to throw away the return ticket because he and his wife now want me to stay with them."

Violet had spoken in her usual quiet matter-of-fact sort of way. Daphne just stared up at her sister from her pink, floral-patterned pillow. The woman's mouth hung open, and with her stone-grey eyes she resembled a fishmonger's cod. Violet thought that Daphne's bed cap was uncommonly like a tea cosy, and with her hand she covered the faint smile that hovered on her lips. A cod with a tea cosy for a hat!

Daphne remained speechless.

"You'll find plenty of food in the fridge," Violet continued. "Mr Freeman will deliver the groceries as usual. Mrs Williams will see to most things, and I'm sure you'll enjoy the meals on wheels." .

The elder sister's cod-fish face went through a series of Rowlandson cartoon contortions as she tried to make sense of what she'd just heard.

"Violet!"

Daphne had finally found her tongue

"Violet, I don't think I heard you properly. I thought you said…"

"Yes," said Violet calmly, "I'm off to stay with my son in America. I have three grand-children and one great grand-child, and I can't wait to see them. It's all so exciting, don't you think?"

Daphne was not used to having questions put to her, but this one was simply preposterous. Her cod-fish mouth opened and closed, offering little in the way of sound other than a meaningless squeak. It wasn't until Violet had left the room and closed the bedroom door that the fire-works really started.

"*Violet, come back in here at once!*"

Violet re-entered her sister's room.

"Violet, what on earth were you saying? If this is one of your dreamy little fantasies I think it's in bad taste. Very bad indeed! And what do you think father would have said had he heard you talk like that? Shameful! A very distasteful joke, Violet!"

Violet took the liberty of sitting down on the edge of her sister's bed as she gave Daphne the whole story. She told her sister how she'd become pregnant towards the end of the war, when she was just seventeen, explaining, in response to Daphne's expression of bewilderment, that those three months away, supposedly doing teacher training, were spent with a close friend of their mother prior to the baby's birth. Their mother had made the adoption arrangements, despite her poor state of health, when it became clear that Violet would not be able to keep the child. The pain of having her own baby taken from her was, said Violet, indescribable, but her mother helped her through it all. Violet paused. Daphne's mouth had remained open all the time, still unable to believe a word of what she was hearing. She was just about to say something, when Violet continued:

"And yes," she said, "I do know who the father was. We were going to marry when the war was over, but he never even got the chance to know that I was pregnant. He was killed a month before the end of the war. What do you think of that, Daphne? The war destroyed our happiness!"

Daphne visibly flinched at the word 'pregnant'.

"David traced me after his adoptive mother died at the end of last year. There were papers from our mother which his adoptive mother had kept from him all these years. Thankfully the old lady hadn't got rid of them. So that's about it. In a nut shell, so to speak!"

Daphne found her voice again. It was loud and clear.

"*Disgusting!*" she shrieked. "True or not, it's all too disgusting! I don't want to hear about it again. Our father would have been simply appalled!"

Daphne pulled the bed clothes right up to her pimpled chin as though this should somehow emphasise her point.

"Your father, Daphne," said Violet quietly, before leaving her half-sister to her mutterings as she closed the door behind her.

That was the last time Violet saw Daphne. As she sat in the airplane bound for Boston, she mused over the previous evening's confrontation with a smile on her face. She was happy, really happy, perhaps for the first time since Alan had died and David had been taken from her. Her son sounded so nice from their talks over the telephone.

She pulled out the envelope from her bag and extracted the photograph of David. Every bit as handsome as Alan, the American airman she should have married. How ironic that David should end up in America after his adoptive parents emigrated in the early fifties. Alan had promised her such a wonderful life in America. Their love was so intense that she always knew there could never have been any one else for her, particularly as a part of Alan, their son David, was alive somewhere in the world. Until then, Violet never knew that her mother had sent details about herself to the adoption agency for forwarding to the baby's adoptive parents.

Violet took from the envelope the family tree her mother had drawn up for her grandson to see one day. It showed that a certain Joseph Barrington, who died from tuberculosis at the age of thirty-four in nineteen twenty-nine, the year after Violet was born, was her true father. She was so happy to know that she wasn't a Pringle, after all!

Mrs Crawford's Bereavement

Sally Patricia Gardner

Mrs Crawford had always been a great believer in the power of prayer, but she knew that things had gone too far for that. Gingerly, she pushed back the covers on her side of the bed and let her feet search for her slippers. She knew that it was important to keep warm when you were suffering from shock, especially at her age.

She had known there was something wrong as soon as she woke. Of the two of them, he had been the early riser. It was his stretching and yawning that always woke her. She often chided him, laughing that she wouldn't have minded another undisturbed half an hour in bed, but they both knew she didn't mean it. He would answer her by bending over and kissing her cheek. This morning it had been the silence that roused her.

Resting on the side of the bed for a moment she waited for the pounding of her heart to subside. Then, screwing up her courage, she rose and walked round to Freddie's side of the bed. There was no room for doubt. He must have gone in the small hours as rigor mortis was already setting in. She laid her head beside his on the pillow and let a long sob rack her body. She let her tears run freely down her cheeks as she gently kissed the top of his head.

"Oh, Freddy, my darling, darling boy. How shall I manage without you?" It wasn't even as if he had been ill. Like her, he was a good age, but there had been no particular slowing down, no warning signs. Only last night she had pointed out to him that his favourite telly programme was on this afternoon and she knew he was looking forward to watching it with her. This recollection caused her another paroxysm of sobbing. After a while she carefully arranged the covers round him and smoothed his pillow.

She dressed carefully, choosing a black skirt and jumper. There was no-one to see it, but it seemed appropriate. That was when the realisation hit her that she should think about notifying her family and that she would have to arrange for some kind of funeral. She went down to the kitchen and put the kettle on. It seemed so empty without his cheerful presence. They always started the day with two slices of toast and marmalade each, although she had been careful just to give him a scrape of butter on his since they had been warned that he needed to watch his weight. She couldn't face it today, but conscious that she should eat something, she buttered and slowly ate a piece of bread.

It was so long since she had spoken to her daughter that she had to look up the number. It seemed to go on ringing forever, then her daughter's voice cut in. "Tamsin and Jeremy are unable to talk to you at the moment, but please leave us a message. Thank you." Mrs Crawford replaced the phone. She was certainly not going to leave a message. After all, when had Tamsin last bothered with either of them? Months ago. When she had lived at home she and Freddy had been so close – well, they all had been – but now she had this posh new life they were just an encumbrance, or that was how it felt.

She couldn't remember if Tom was away or not. He was always having to go over to America on business. His job was something she found quite impenetrable, to do with computers. But she knew that he would want to know. And he would care. Yes, Tom would certainly grieve. He had always been such a good son.

She had his mobile number. That also asked her to leave a message. But this time she did.

Trying, unsuccessfully, not to cry, she told him what had happened. "I know that you loved him as much as he loved you, son," she finished, "I'd like you to see him before…" and here it was all too much for her and she put the phone down quickly.

Then she slowly climbed the stairs again and went and lay down beside him, looking into his dear face.

Several hours later she was woken by gentle hands shaking her. "Hi, Mum," said Tom. He put his arms round her and held her close. "You're cold," he said, "I've got the boys with me and we've lit the sitting room fire. You must come down and get warm. Is it alright if the boys come up and see…?"

She nodded. Of course her grandsons would want to say goodbye. She had expected that.

Tom led her into the sitting room and sat her by the fire. Mark and Andrew came and put their arms round her and she could see that Mark, the younger, had been crying. Tom said: "I'll just go up with the boys Mum, and then we'll do all the necessary. We did a bit while you were asleep."

When they came back downstairs Mark came and gave her another hug. "He looks so peaceful, Gran."

Then they got out her boots and warm coat and scarf, because although the evenings were drawing out again and it was still quite light, it was very cold. Mark held her arm as they went into the garden and she was startled to realise that he was taller than her now.

They had got everything ready under the forsythia tree. She always kept the old recliner there in the summer for him. It was definitely his favourite spot in their small garden.

Tom and Andrew carried him down between them. Mark took the blanket off the recliner and tucked it gently round him. They kept the ceremony short, and then they went back into the house, because Mrs Crawford was shivering.

"We'll stay with you for a bit, Gran," said Mark. "It's his favourite programme on in a minute, isn't it?" She squeezed his hand and nodded. "There's some cake in the tin, and make some more tea for us, Tom, there's a love."

He did. And then the four of them settled down together to watch *One man and his Dog*. And to remember, with a little laughter and yet more tears, how Freddy had always barked at the television as he watched the competitors go through their paces.

'Dingo' and the RWF

Robert Jenkins

Between 1978 and 1980, I served with the Royal Military Police in Londonderry, Northern Ireland. My unit was stationed at the old US Navy base at Clooney in the Waterside, but we were responsible for patrolling within the City walls on the opposite bank of the river Foyle.

The City side of Londonderry was the responsibility of the roulemont infantry battalion whose companies were dispersed amongst Security Force bases at Strand Road, Masonic, Creggan and Fort George.

We were all engaged in internal security duties and the relationship between ourselves and the infantry was far different to other theatres, but even so, it remained a bit cool.

Then, around October, 1978 the 1st Battalion Royal Welch Fusiliers took over and the picture altered. They quickly won our respect and we rated them very highly. They had just the right qualities for winning the hearts and minds of the locals – as far as that was possible – but they were really professional troops, too.

It was about that time that we noticed 'Dingo'. He was a mongrel dog who looked a bit like an Australian dingo, hence his name, I suppose. He lived in the base at Fort George and would accompany the RWF on patrol, switching from one patrol to another as the fancy took him. The story went that he had been knocked down by a 'Pig' (a Humber one ton armoured troop carrier) and taken for veterinary treatment by the patrol responsible. He recovered and lived thereafter at the base, requiring a second period of recovery after he got caught up in a riot and had his fur burnt in places, by the effects of a petrol bomb.

He was a scabby looking dog, but the Taffs of C Company at Fort George looked after him well and just as a dog can bring strangers to talk in other situations, he got us and the Fusiliers chatting and waving to each other. He even started including our patrols in his companionship duties and woe betides the fool who tried to hurt him just to spite us or the soldiers! It used to make me smile to see him leave a foot patrol to chase after a Landrover borne mobile patrol. You'd hear the guys in the back telling the driver to slow down to let Dingo aboard and he would then leap up and sit quite happily looking out of the back, until he got fed up and leapt out, having spotted another foot patrol.

My memory of those months is of a particularly good rapport with C Company 1RWF – largely thanks to Dingo. It was a great privilege to work alongside such a fine regiment.

On Valentine's Day, 1979, one of their young officers (Lieutenant Steven Kirby, age 22) was murdered by a sniper whilst leading a patrol in the vicinity of the Foyle Bridge. It was only a couple of weeks before the end of their tour. The identity of the gunman was quickly ascertained, but by then he had fled across the boarder to Letterkenny. One afternoon however, he was thought to have resurfaced in the Creggan and the Brigade radio net burst into life with a multitude of RWF call signs co-ordinating a search for him – every one of them speaking in Welsh! The Brigade Watch Keeper who monitored the net and activities in his patch was going mad with frustration, but we knew what was going on. Our own Officer Commanding (who would one day become the Provost Marshal) was keen for us to help if we could, but sadly the sniper wasn't found – which was very lucky for him.

Just a few days before C Company departed, we showed a side of the RMP that soldiers rarely saw. With the full blessing of our OC, we sent a snatch squad across to Fort George and kidnapped their OC (whose name was Major Cheney-Williams I think) from his own room. Although initially somewhat alarmed – as you might expect – he was a good sport and came quietly. With the hostage safely back across the river, a ransom demand was made to C Company Operations Room. It went something like this.

"Morning, Boyo. It's the RMP at Clooney, here. Don't worry if you can't find your OC, we thought we'd give him a break from you 'orrible lot, so we've kidnapped him and fetched him back with us. If you want him returned safely, it will cost you your company pennant, to be delivered by whoever comes to collect him."

"Oh… you've got the OC, is it? Ah well, we never did like him much anyway. You keep him." Click. *Buzzzzzzz.*

We thought that was a bit unfair, but the devious Welsh devils had only just begun to play with us. The previous evening, one of their patrols had dropped off a member of our Women's Royal Army Corps searchers – and she'd been blabbing about things that she's heard were afoot.

Consequently, as the patrol stopped to load their rifles on their way out, one of their number slipped away unseen to the big American flag pole at the entrance of our base and stole our Corps flag from it. The flag was never ordinarily raised or lowered, since to form any such pattern of activity was to invite a bullet. Thus, none of us had even noticed its disappearance – until C Company Ops room rang us back.

"Hullo, Monkeys. Taffy here. We've had a chat and we've decided that it wouldn't be Christian to leave the OC with a bunch of heathens like you, so you bring him back and we'll return your Corps flag to you. It makes a lousy tablecloth, anyway."

We were sorry to see them leave Londonderry and before much longer, our role changed to taking control of the border crossing points in the Londonderry enclave, so we never saw Dingo again and I don't know what happened to him. He was a good dog though and I shall always associate him with that fine body of men who wore a white hackle in their berets.

THE LAST HOUSECARL

Tony Brindle

James turned the green stone over between his fingers.

His chest boiled to a wound inflicted from the sword of a French Knight. Blood bubbled freely from its surface. The stump of his right arm, secured in a tourniquet bled dark clots into dirty rags used to dress it.

He remained determined to hide any trace of fear from his captors.

"I am a Housecarl." He whispered. "A Nobleman's Warrior. The King's own Captain of Warriors." He smiled and looked into the dark eyes of the Conqueror.

The Conqueror pursed his lips and looked sideways at him in judgement. "You are James, correct."

James nodded once.

"Captain and first Housecarl to Harold Godwinson?"

"I am Lord." James stiffened slightly. He felt William the Bastard's eyes study him.

"Is it true? The Royal Housecarl's make a blood oath to die in defence of their King?"

"It is true, Lord."

"Hmm." William sighed. "A brave man, your King. I would have you tell me of his final moments. I will know it all." He turned to one of his servants. "Bring him water."

His cold face dissolved and James noticed the first flicker of weariness in the Conqueror's expression. James thought of Harold and of his men. He cleared his parched throat and coughed blood. "I will Lord. I am but a humble Housecarl and my words are simple things. Yet my account is the equal of any Greek Iliad."

The corner of the Conqueror's eyebrow climbed up his forehead. "You know the Iliad's? Then you are no common soldier."

James stared beyond the Conqueror at the tapestry walls of his captor's temporary royal enclosure. "I will tell you of the bravery of my men, and of the glorious moments of the last English King."

"In your own time, Captain of Housecarls."

James took a deep breath. "Like the Iliad's we fought in the shade of thousands of arrows and, like the Spartans, we were past caring. Our shield wall had crumbled and the last of our men stood huddled at the top of the hill. We spat at the approaching charge of French Knights…"

"Surround and protect your King!" James shouted his orders to the remaining Housecarl contingent. The Royal bodyguards, no more now than twenty in number closed ranks. They formed a wall of shields and horses around Harold, determined to honour the pledge of loyalty to their King.

"I will let my men see their King." Harold pressed his charger forward.

James took the reins and nudged at his Kings charger with his own. Both horses snapped at each other.

"You, my Lord, will stay here." James nodded to another Housecarl. The man detached his horse from the shield wall and began to canter along the crest of the hill.

Arrows continued to rain down and thud into their shields. James watched the Housecarl reach the end of the English lines untouched. His square set jaw and resemblance to King Harold was uncanny. They cheered him and waved. Edward, the eldest of the Royal Housecarl regiment exchanged a little banter with men who knew they were about to die. He turned his mount and began his return.

James watched the trajectory of a lone arrow; detached from the others, it began a slow descent toward the Housecarl. At the last moment, Edward looked up toward the incoming threat as it buried itself into his face. James looked on as Edward rocked back, forth and to one side. Edward screamed. The remaining foot soldiers saw it too and they groaned. At the bottom of the hill the French foot soldiers had seen it and a ripple of cheers echoed through their ranks.

James watched in awe as the man regained control and cantered back to the Housecarl encirclement. An arrow protruded deep from within Edwards's eye socket and blood covered his face.

Peppered by a wave of arrows, the front legs of his horse

collapsed. The Housecarl fell forward and landed near James's feet, sending up sods of blood stained mud and turf. The Housecarls gathered the injured man into the centre with their king.

Harold took hold of his Housecarl and cradled his head and shoulders in his arms. "My King." James heard Edward whisper. "I regret to inform you that the end is upon us."

The arrows stopped falling. For a few moments James thought he heard birdsong coming from a distant tree line. Then the ground began to vibrate. James glanced around his shield and down the hill. A wall of snarling, foaming, horse borne death began to charge up the hill toward them.

James noticed his King turn in his saddle. "My loyal Housecarls, England's blood flows down this hill. As mine will soon mix with yours; know this. I promise in the presence of our Lord that today we die defending our own soil as brothers. We will stand at the feet of St Peter, and the gates of heaven will open."

"I'm English. I piss on heaven. Give me a whore and a warm blanket any day." One of the men countered.

The King laughed with them all. "Thomas, you never were a God-fearing man."

"My Lord King, I know nothing of frigid angels and pious merchants shaking in prayer. So let the French have Heaven, and leave an Englishman to get drunk, and lead his horse through Hell!" Thomas raised his sword in the air and howled.

The King continued to smile. "I can only imagine the dread in the minds of those Knights. They charge toward us and see us speared with arrows. Yet in the face of death, we laugh at them."

The hooves of the French chargers crested the hill. James saw them raise their swords and press their horses into further speed.

"My Housecarls, they are upon us. Our bones will bleach this hill of England and our blood will cover them in shame. With me my brothers, this day, we will drink a toast of Kentish ale. In paradise!"

The French Knights fell on them, slicing, cutting and thrusting. The Royal Housecarls wreaked bitter havoc and held them off. The first French Knights rode past, not one remained uninjured. They slowed their horses. On the turn, the remaining infantry soldiers threw their bodies onto the swords of the Knights and sacrificing their numbers, cut them down.

Another wave of Knights charged. Armed with Lance and mace, they skewered the Housecarls, carrying several forward like speared fish. The Knights behind charged the thinning line again with the sword.

James saw his King fight like a man possessed of evil spirits. He cut, slashed, and parried. However, a French Noble, dressed in red lacquered armour drew his sword arm high in the air for the killing blow. James saw the danger and charged forward, raising his sword arm to parry the strike. The Frenchman's sword dropped and swept with practised skill and James's arm spun in the air showering them with blood, severed high above the elbow.

King Harold looked to his first Housecarl and smiled. Their horses buckled, their knees unstrung by axe and mace, they fell to the ground embraced.

Dazed, James lay as French knights dragged the king to one side and surrounded him. In a frenzied bloodlust they hacked him to pieces. At his side lay his Kings sword. Its damaged hilt loosely housed a green emerald stone. Whilst the Knights were busy with his King, James picked the green stone and in his good hand he clenched it. A shadow fell over him and he looked up. A French Knight grimaced over him and spittle drooled from his mouth. With casual indifference he plunged his sword into James's chest.

The Conqueror placed a hand on James's shoulder. "So, your King did not die to the arrow?"

"No Lord. He did not. He died fighting."

William took a deep breath and blew out hard. He looked away in thought.

"It is done Lord." James exhaled and his body relaxed. His hand loosened its grip on the green stone and it fell. It rolled on the floor and stopped at the foot of the Conqueror.

For several seconds the Conqueror stared down at it, then at him. He swept his hand over the glazed empty eyes of The Housecarl. "Go to your last English King. Do what you English do best, drink, fight and make merry with your women. You have earned it. For my part, I shall offer prayers in thanks and deliverance. This land, my land, will know the names of the warriors at the blood lakes of Senlac Hill."

Saddened, William glanced across at his Sergeant at arms. "My Lord." He hesitated. "Shall we at least, give this English warrior, a proper burial?"

In silence William studied the hanging tapestries. An idea sparked to life in his mind. He looked into the eyes of the man sitting across from him as he spoke, "Yes."

SNAPPED

Kristin Young (age 14)

My heart, my brain, my life stopped the moment the words came from his mouth.

"The Army? Jake, you can't be serious," said my mother in disbelief.

Though she said nothing else I knew her thoughts, I could see them in her eyes. The worry in her eyes mirrored my own.

"I've already thought it through and it's perfect for me," he replied as easy as if we were talking about something funny that happened at school.

My mother's eyes were not the only ones that spoke unsaid words. I could see everything as easy as if I was looking directly into his head. Excitement, pride, hope, eagerness. I could also see every reason as well. I couldn't find it in me to be as serious as this conversation was.

"Ha! The military would chew you up and spit you out," I laughed teasingly. Then I suddenly found myself wondering if Jake had been planning on this. I had assumed that the sudden interest in taking weight lifting as a gym for school was to impress girls, but now I felt myself back tracking.

"Listen," said Jake as if I hadn't spoken (something I was grateful for). "If I get into the Air Force they'll pay for me to get my pilot's licenses at any college I choose, plus it's an automatic acceptance."

I knew it before he'd even said it. The military was his way of getting to fly without massive college fees. But was that it; or were there ulterior motives and this was just his cover story?

"I know we don't have a ton of money," began my father, "but that doesn't mean you have to join the military."

My world was falling. I didn't want to admit it but I could see the perks of his plans. Free aviation training, an automatic acceptance to any school he wanted to go to, knowing you'll have a job immediately out of college, and knowing you job was secure for six years (something people no longer seem to take for granted). It was all there for him. He started taking aviation training when he was fourteen or fifteen years old, and ever since we knew that's where he'd end up.

But whether he couldn't see them or was simply ignoring them, the negatives were all there as well. I could hear my parents' conversation; talking about the boot camps and the extra training, and his other options he'd have a bigger passion for. But I truly couldn't hear, nothing was processing. All I could see was a plane going down in flames, dropping bombs, and other images I will never get out of my head if I live sixty more years.

"You wouldn't last two days," I joked, but the words had more meaning and fear behind them than anyone would have ever guessed. I couldn't allow myself to take this seriously because I didn't want to think about this seriously. As I knew that every soldier who went in had the chance of never coming back again. I pushed these thoughts from my head as I said, "Jake, you have to get up early, eat what you're served when you're served, and listen to others and do what they say without comments. Not your favorite things," I teased. "Not to mention boot camp," I added.

"It's six years!" said our mom, and I thought I heard almost a plead in her voice. "You have to think about this very carefully, after you sign up there's no getting out. You'd be stuck for six years somewhere you may hate, or you could even get all your licenses and then get assigned to be an engineer or something similar. You may not even get to fly going this route."

"That's six years of knowing my job's secure. Something I wouldn't get anywhere else, especially working for Delta or Comair," he replied.

"Mom, I'm going to go take a shower," I interrupted, clearing my spot at the dinner table.

"Okay," she answered, it didn't even seem like she was paying attention. I could see the concentration on her face. Trying to find something to make him waver, anything. I knew Jake would need a lot of convincing to get our family to agree with his decision, assuming he actually had a chance. I looked at my parents faces and thought about my own thoughts. He had no chance. If he made this decision I would be proud of him, supportive, provided there was no way out. But I could never agree with it, because although I would never let it show I couldn't handle it. Not knowing, questioning, and worrying.

I hardly had time to leave the kitchen before my face was wet enough to look like my shower was already through. Six years. Please Lord, not him. Not him. I don't know what I'd do if I lost him.

That's when I had to turn on the shower. So no one could hear my heart snapping to pieces.

A Place Of Safety
(The Cup And Saucer Tree)

A R (David) Lewis

For more than seventy years, I have kept secret my faith in that beautiful tree, and in all that time it has never failed me.

In times of great stress, and sometimes great danger, I simply climb up into its branches, letting my mind absorb its magic, and I know I am safe in its embrace.

As a small boy looking up into its thickly woven branches, I realised that in some way my life, and the tree would be bonded together. It was our destiny.

Standing up from the hedgerow, the round smooth trunk held up the saucer shaped base, with its closely knit , almost impenetrable branches. This in turn held the full shape of the cup, creating a perfect cup and saucer image in a living breathing natural tree.

How I longed to climb into its centre. I knew that when that was achieved, I would be in my own private castle, my tower, my refuge, my place of sanctuary, where nothing could cause me harm. A green haven of peace.

It would be my secret, kept hidden in my mind. My World shared only with nature, and perhaps a nesting Finch or Thrush. We would be safe, encompassed in green caressing leaves, secure like a child in a mothers embrace.

Despite all set backs, a period in Hospital, an arm broken on two occasions, I never lost that burning desire. One day soon I would fulfil my dream.

Even before that great day the tree dominated my thoughts. At four years old, I sat in bed in that old Tubercular Hospital at Gobowen, out on the verandah of the open ended wards, snowflakes blowing in on the foot of the bed, I was oblivious to icy winter winds, fits of coughing, horrible medicenes, huge spoonfuls of Cod Liver Oil. I just thought and dreamed of my beautiful tree, knowing that I would recover, be reunited with that secret world.

Eventually the time came, I knew that moment of glory was to hand, the tree would be climbed that weekend, or at least by the following Bank Holiday Monday.

I remember the intense excitement, the anticipation of what was to come. Chores were carried out quickly, and cheerfully.

My Mother became suspicious, I heard her remark, "That little devil is up to something."

Oh yes, I was, and a lot higher up than she thought.

My first attempt despite the planning was a complete failure. It became apparent that during my wait to get strong enough, I had also grown considerably .Alternate routes to the summit would have to be explored.

Eventually the first part was achieved, I was in the saucer, even that brought great delight, and spurred me on to greater efforts.

Squirming and wriggling my way up into the cup, I lay there my mind and body overcome with emotion.

Every thing I had dreamed of was at lat true. The sense of achievement, and above all a feeling of complete safety, I was alone, as one with this living breathing tree, almost a part of nature itself, nothing could possibly harm me.

After all this time, scraped knees, scratched hands, and a torn jersey seem such a small price to have paid for such high rewards.

Snow Boots

Joanne Hall

The German soldiers arrived with the sunset, marching into the yard in a wavering line. They stood waiting while their commander spoke to Svetlana's father. She peeped around the door frame, watching them. How straight they stood, how proud in their ragged uniforms. Defeat had not bowed their heads. She crept closer to eavesdrop on the commander, conversing with her father in halting Russian. Her father was scowling.

"You can stay one night. One!" Ivan held up a finger, making sure he was understood. "Leave the guns outside. You can collect them in the morning."

The commander issued a sharp order, and there was a clattering as the Germans dropped their heavy rifles. One of the strangers hunkered down to watch over them. The rest scattered, their discipline swept away. Ivan was still talking to the commander as Olga and Natalya emerged from two of the huts on the opposite side of the yard, curious, casting nervous glances at the pile of guns. Svetlana watched her father reassure them, knowing they would be forced to defer to his will. Ivan was the only man of working age in the collective, since the younger, fitter men had marched away to war and never come back.

Svetlana's mother appeared at her elbow. "What's going on, child?"

"Father says the Germans can stay."

Marie sighed. "Your father would do anything to spit in Stalin's eye, even helping our enemies. Have they brought any food?"

Svetlana shrugged. The soldiers were much more interesting than her mother's domestic worries, and she was bored of hearing about Stalin. To her father, the collective was a prison, but to Svetlana it was home. She couldn't remember living anywhere else.

The German commander issued another instruction. His men teamed into pairs or trios, and one pair headed purposefully towards the doorway where Svetlana lurked. She backed away, slowly, into the kitchen, watching in silence as the men took seats at the table. One was short and squat, with thick brows and a protuberant lower lip. He kept his eyes down, making no contact with anyone. The other, younger man reminded Svetlana of the forbidden bible stories her mother had told her since she was a babe in arms. She liked the ones about Saint Michael the Archangel best, slaying the dragon with his flaming sword. She had dreamed of him, tall and blond, gentle but powerful. The other German, tucking into her mother's thin turnip stew as if it was the finest dessert, was the Archangel Michael come to earth. He was tall and fair, with blue eyes that gleamed over his sunken cheeks. He saw her looking, and smiled. His teeth were yellow, but his grin was broad and welcoming. Svetlana felt the heat rise in her face as he tapped himself on the chest.

"Wilhelm." He pointed to her.

"Svetlana."

"Svetlana, don't bother the man." Marie fluttered between the table and the stove, picking up pots, laying them aside again, with many anxious glances at the strangers. "I think you should go upstairs now."

"She doesn't need to go upstairs," Ivan said, just as quickly. "I want her down here, with us." He called her over to him and hugged her awkwardly with his shortened arm, empty sleeve flapping. He ate with his right hand, watching the Germans constantly, and she wondered if he regretted his decision.

The meal over, the dark German rolled a thin cigarette. Wilhelm rose and began clearing the bowls from the table. "Thank you," he said, in Russian, with a small bow towards Marie. She stood with her back against the stove, clutching a wooden spatula to her chest as if it was a weapon, and made no reply.

The table cleared, Wilhelm shuffled his chair closer to the fire, and stretched out his long, skinny legs, closing his eyes. With his lashes resting on his cheeks and the firelight giving a ruddy tone to his pale skin, he looked more angelic than ever. Svetlana crept closer, ignoring her father's muttered warning.

She sat at Wilhelm's feet and stared at his boots. The leather was cracked across the toes, and the sole was coming away on both heels. The laces, knotted tightly, were thin and stringy. Wilhelm, noticing her interest, leant forward to untie them, and the left lace snapped. He sighed, removed the remains from the boot, and held it out to her. "For your hair," he said.

With a hesitant glance at her father, Svetlana took the lace. The brush of Wilhelm's hand against hers sent a jolt like lightening up her arm. She blushed, but he didn't seem to notice as he eased the broken boots from his swollen feet. His grey woollen socks had been ripped and darned so many times they were just a mass of tangled stitching, raw heels and toes poking through like fat white maggots. He pulled off his wet socks and let them fall, extending his feet towards the fire. Svetlana hardly noticed the smell. She was looking at the blisters, the calluses, the fine golden hair that sprouted from the tops of his toes.

"Daddy, how far is it to the border?"

"On foot?" Ivan considered. "About four days, in the snow. Come away from there now, and help your mother."

Four days. Four days over snow, in boots that leaked and rubbed with every step. It most be agony for her poor Archangel. Who knew how far he had walked already? Maybe all the way from Moscow! The thought brought tears to her eyes as she imagined those poor soldiers, knowing they had lost, marching mile after mile through the bitter Russian winter in boots of rotten leather, with never a murmur of complaint. Not like Russian boys, always moaning about something. The Germans, in defeat, were true heroes.

Marie leaned over to her. "Don't cry," she whispered. "I know you're scared, but they'll be gone in the morning. Try to stay out of their way until then, though. It's not just guns that make a man dangerous."

Svetlana forced a smile. "I think I'm just tired, mother. Do you mind if I go up to bed?"

Her mother regarded her anxiously. "You look a little flushed. Are you feeling all right?"

"I'm fine, honestly."

Marie hugged her impetuously. "We'll keep you safe, my dear. You know that, don't you?"

"I know!" Svetlana struggled free from her arms, hating to be treated like a child in front of Wilhelm. She climbed swiftly to the loft-bedroom she shared with her parents, had shared with her older brothers before they went away to war. She imagined Anatoly and Boris without their boots, trudging through the snow, and then the idea struck her. She could give Wilhelm her father's *valenki*.

The high felt boots that kept Ivan's feet dry and warm even in the cruellest winters were not in their usual place in the trunk at the foot of her parents bed. Twenty minutes of sweaty, frustrated searching led eventually to their discovery, beneath the false panel in the bottom of the wardrobe, where her mother kept the bible and a few precious items of jewellery that had belonged to Svetlana's great-grandmother. Now she knew where they were, she would have to wait until her parents were asleep. She anticipated the row that would erupt if her father caught her giving his valuable snow boots to a German.

"To each according to his need," she muttered as she replaced the panel. And who was more in need than poor Wilhelm?

Later that night, when the snores of her parents assured her they would not hear, Svetlana lifted the *valenki* from their hiding place, and climbed down the ladder with them tucked awkwardly under her arm. Wilhelm slept where she had left him, in front of the dying fire, head tipped back and his chest rising and falling gently. His dour companion was passed out with his head on the table, one arm stretching for the empty vodka bottle. Her father, she remembered, had been saving that lonely bottle for her brothers return.

She crept up to Wilhelm and tapped him daringly on the shoulder. He sat up with a grunt, groping at his hip for a weapon that wasn't there, until his bleary eyes focussed on her. He relaxed, smiling that golden smile.

"Svetlana."

The way he said her name set off strange, uncomfortable feelings in the pit of her stomach. She tried not to imagine what it would feel like if he kissed her. When the men left the collective, she had been nine, and too young for kissing.

"I got you these." She held up the *valenki*, a black shadow in the firelight. How much of what she said did he even understand? "For you." She pointed. "They're my father's, so hush!"

"Hush!" He mimicked her gesture, pressing his finger to his lips. "For me?"

She nodded.

"Thank you, Svetlana." He poked the fire into renewed life and tried on the *valenki*, twisting his legs to admire them under the blaze. They fitted well, just a shade too large. "Thank you." He raised her hand to his lips and kissed it. She felt the rough brush of his stubble, the wetness of his mouth, and panic rushed through her, driving out the warm glow. She snatched her hand back and raced for the ladder, heart pounding, hearing Wilhelm's low chuckle behind her. It was a long time before she slept again that night, and when she did her dreams were full of angels, with flaming swords and soft, red mouths.

"Wake up, sleepy! You've missed breakfast." Marie's cold hand on her bare toes jerked Svetlana roughly from her troubled sleep. She sat up in a hurry.

"Have the Germans gone, mother?"

"They're just going. I saved some porridge for you. And stay out of your father's way. He wanted to go hunting after they've gone, and he can't find his *valenki*." Her expression clouded for a second, then cleared. "I'm sure they'll turn up," she said brightly. Svetlana squirmed internally, but said nothing.

Ivan sat at the table, toying with the empty vodka bottle. His face was as black as a winter night. Ignoring her mother's warning, eager to make amends, Svetlana slipped into the seat beside him and hugged his truncated arm.

"Don't worry, father," she said. "I'm sure Olga has some valenki you can borrow."

His eyes, when they turned on her, were those of a man lying at the bottom of a deep pit. "You don't understand," he said, "and why should you? If they found them –"

"Don't talk about it!" Marie squeaked, rattling the breakfast pans.

"Don't talk about what?" But Svetlana's question was cut off by the appearance in the doorway of the German commander. He saluted her father, bowed to her mother, and spoke, slow and halting, to them both. He was asking Ivan to come with his men, to show them the way back to the main road.

Ivan rose slowly. There was no colour in his face, and he reached for his galoshes like a man having trouble moving his limbs. Marie clutched the front of the stove, mouthing a silent prayer.

"Don't look like that." Svetlana could see how much effort was behind her father's smile. "I'll be back in an hour. You," he kissed Svetlana lightly on the cheek, and she felt him trembling, "be good for your mother while I'm gone."

The commander held the door open for him, and ushered him politely into the yard, letting the door click shut behind them. At that soft sound, whatever power was holding Marie upright collapsed and she sank to the table, head in hands. "Dear God in Heaven, what will we do?"

"What's wrong?" This sudden collapse frightened Svetlana beyond all reason. "Father's only taking them to the road. He'll be back soon. Why are you crying?"

Marie wiped her eyes. "Your father thinks the Germans found his *valenki*."

"What's that got to do with anything?"

"When the Germans invaded, they confiscated all the *valenki* for their own men. They said the partisans were using them, and anyone caught with *valenki* must be a partisan. It's as bad as being caught with a gun, and the punishment is the same."

Oh dear god, the *valenki*! What had she done? Svetlana leapt up from the table with a cry of pain. "I didn't know!"

"Svetlana! Where are you going?"

She rushed out into the yard, hardly feeling the chill on her bare feet. The Germans had already vanished, taking her father with them, but they had left a broad trail from her to follow. Out of the gate, and over the small ridge into the valley below.

She was halfway up the ridge when the rifle cracked, echoing in the winter stillness. Stumbling and crying, Svetlana crested the low rise. Her father lay face-down in the snow, his blood a startling bloom of red against the whiteness. She skidded down the rise towards him and flung herself next to his warm body, howling in grief. As she struggled to lift him, all she could see was the blood, and the footprints leading away from the scene, the heavy, ridged prints of the German army boots. Mixed in with them, sometimes overlaying them, sometimes side-by-side, were the lighter, flatter prints of her father's *valenki*.

THIRTEEN MINUTES

Lillie Rottenm (Age 15)

My back was aching, I was unbearably cold and I was sure my
feet had lost all sensation, yet I refused to move. Moving would
make it real. I looked again at the place where she had dropped.
Just two hundred and thirteen minutes ago she had dropped there.
Those first thirteen minutes took every ounce of life out of my
soul which had been left after the war and terror that devastated
the landscapes of my homeland.

No, those thirteen minutes were the worst. They made the
shooting and the gun fire seem a symphony in the background.
They made the destruction around me, which crumbled and
shook with every accent in the symphony, which reached for a
crescendo, a dream. Those minutes made me remember the fact
that I couldn't recall a time when there was colour and happiness
in my village – all I could remember were men who weren't my
father, battering their fists against the door. I could remember
nothing of a life of peace – now there was only constant uncer-
tainty and fear.

My only measurement of time was the church clock: I had
no measurement of seasons, though my mother claimed that it
was winter. I knew no months and their clichés: to me all seasons
looked the same, all with a bleakness and a terror which I experienced every second. I knew that another world, another time
existed, a time where men didn't drink themselves senseless in
the café with their dirty uniforms and twisted jokes. There was a
time when my mother smiled, I had a father and a brother, and we
didn't need to run every time we heard the gun fire of the biggest
guns start up again.

A man had shot her. He had been in a different uniform to
everyone else. They all wore grey, and they promised to protect us.
But this man, he wore green. She pushed me out of the way when
he came towards us. I fell against the wall and my head started
bleeding, but I was quiet and curled up, pretending, like Mamam
always told me, like I wasn't there. The man shot her in the legs

when she saw he wasn't a grey man and tried to run. Grey men were nice, we had learnt. They had come to our village and had treated me kindly, though they rarely gave me food . They patted me on the head, told me I would become a beautiful women and then told me tales of their homeland, which was different to ours. The men were cordial to my mother, but only because their captain reprimanded them when they weren't.

Men ran by. The clatter of their loud footsteps should have warned me of their coming; I had heard them but I had been too scared to listen, so when they ran by the alley their pounding footsteps seemed amplified. I looked at the men and was relieved to find them wearing grey.

The grey men, who had resided in our village for almost four years, had left for a month or two. Mamam said that that meant the shooting, the killing and the war were almost over, but now they were back, bringing their gunfire with them.

The men ran past the entrance to the alley continually, and as the minutes wore on I recognised the odd man. Different groups came to our village and rested here for four or five days. These were made up of about fifty men. I remembered the captains, who wore eagles on their helmets, I remember the nice men, who gave me a sip of their drink which tasted disgusting or let me wear their caps for a day. From the crowed of running men I picked out some of the men who had asked me to pray for them, some of their friends and some men who told me of their losses.

I watched, fascinated, as the line of men seemed never ending. They ran in pairs, their rifles and packs slung over their shoulders, tins attached to their rucksacks rattling as they ran. Their panting was almost inaudible over the thump of their heavy boots against the cobbled street, though after listening to their boots slapping in the puddles from the spring rain. I could hear the anger and the fear in the panting.

I started counting the seconds again, using the beat of the men's footsteps as my measurement. There seemed to be an endless line.

Slowly the panting of the men became more audible and the running became slower as the end of the line approached. The last unit was lead by an old man.

I knew this man very well. His unit was the first to sit in our café and talk to us. He had a bushy moustache and a kind face, and many of his men were from a place near France. He spoke French well, though he taught me some German words so I could communicate with his men. Mamam had forbid me to speak any German, but although the language was harder to learn than I thought I liked talking to the men, so I carried on learning it.

We children had a nickname for him, because he was here in the beginning I hadn't been the only child then. But after the gunfire faded into the background, like birdsong in summer, families moved away. Soon the only people left were the family owning the cafe, the old couple, Monsieur and Madame Grielé, and my mother and I. The only family we had lived in Strasbourg, which was on the other side. We called him General Oiseau because of the giant bird on his helmet.

I was cold and in my desperation for help, I feebly called his name.

He didn't even look up from his tired trod, though one man did. I knew this man from seeing – he was one of the thoughtful men who sat at the back of the café, not drinking anything but coffee and a vacant look on his face as he wrote another letter. He had smiled at me once or twice but never been as engaging as the other men.

He saw me and stopped abruptly, calling to his superior. The whole band of men came to a halt while I cursed myself for calling at all. The man slowly advanced down the alley, muttering things to calm me. I was too cold to run even if I wanted to, but I was glad of his kindness.

"*Mädchen?*" the man's voice was soft and I nodded feebly. "Come here." He lifted my body into his arms and brought me to General Oiseau, who inspected and recognised me.

General Oiseau examined me, concerned. "'*Sophie, où est ton mere*? Where is your mother ?*"

I shivered, remembering those thirteen minutes, while the grey man clutching me whispered something to General Oiseau, pointing in the direction of the alleyway.

I knew enough German to understand the men's odd words, so I concentrated hard and tried to remember everything that General Oiseau had taught me. "… we do?" the grey man had just said, hitching me up in his arms. The jolt ran through my bones and made me shiver.

"*Weiss ich doch nicht!*" General Oiseau looked back at the alleyway and then into the direction the other troops had disappeared to. How am I supposed to know? General Oiseau had taught me to say that to any soldier if they asked me anything about the war. It would keep me safe, he promised.

"*Wir fallen zurück. Nimm das Kind. Wir lassen sie beim nächsten Bauernhof.*" The grey man saluted before thanking the captain and going back in to the line. A smile was on his dirty face, like he was triumphant. I hoped it was good news. I knew what 'Bauernhof' meant – I used to live on one. Were they planning to bring me home? But I would be all alone! I shivered again and the grey man looked at me in concern.

He examined my dirty dress in concern before asking me, in perfect French, whether I was cold. I was too numb to feel anything, so I just shook my head, but he chose not to believe me and took a flea bitten blanket out of his bag. He wrapped me in it like a baby and I felt comforted. At General Oiseau's command the men started running again, and as I jolted with them I couldn't believe my luck. I was being saved by this kind man, who had even given me this blanket!

"I have a daughter just like you." He told me, his breath becoming irregular with the strain of the run and my weight. I perked up, surprised and yet wanting to hear more. I had never heard a word from him in the café, so perhaps I would find out why he was quiet. "Her name is Tabitha."

"Tabitha?" I tried and he laughed.

"It's an English name. She was born before the war. I have a good German name though. My name is Siegfried."

I was too tired to make a sentence so I just pointed at myself. "Sophie." Then I pointed at him. "Siegfried." I made the 'g' soft when I pronounced it, making it sound very French.

"It sounds nicer in French." He stated and I nodded in agreement. Everything was nicer in French. "She's six now. My wife tells me she looks as beautiful everyday and she has my facial expressions. I wouldn't know, though, I've missed four years of her life. Just like your father's missed four years of your life."

I nodded holding up four fingers, showing him the years my father had missed. "*Et mon frère,*" I told him.

"My brother was in the war too. He died at Ypres though, three years ago."

I didn't know the place, but I saw the tears in Siegfried's eyes and I knew it was a sad place. To lose someone, that was hard. To lose someone in battle was harder, especially if the battle won nothing. But to watch someone die was the hardest, and I wanted to tell Siegfried he was lucky he didn't have any thirteen minutes. But I didn't. I kept silent and listened to the irregular breathing of the men around me.

I shivered again as Siegfried ran down a muddy path, jolting me up and down. The jolting soon developed a rocking rhythm to it and then, too exhausted even to think, I fell asleep in Siegfried's arms.

The next village was miles away, but I slept during those minutes, waking up screaming every time I closed my eyes, Siegfried panting German lullabies when I was screaming in fear.

I woke up when the heavy rhythm of Siegfried's breathing slowed and the run he had been at for an endless amount of time ended. I knew what this meant, and through the fog of sleep that still clung to me, I gave an involuntary sob. I didn't want this man to leave me.

He hugged me tight and shushed me as he continued at a walk, and I heard General Oiseau's voice next to my head. I opened my eyes to find General Oiseau falling into step with Siegfried, walking towards an odd cluster of villages, just as grey and forgotten as mine had been.

I looked over Siegfried's shoulder and saw General Oiseau's men waiting patiently, welcoming the rest from their run.

General Oiseau knocked on the first door with authority, though the house turned out to be empty. "*Verdamte Franzosen,*" he murmured under his breath, an insult I did understand. I sniffed, making sure he saw that I had understood his rudeness towards my people.

"Sorry Sophie," he said, smiling, but I was too tired to respond with more than a feeble smile.

We knocked on three doors before some owners answered. A large, elderly woman, looked at me in horror, and addressing me in French asked me what these men had done to me.

General Oiseau assured her that they had done nothing, but until my father returned from war I would need some where to live. The woman took me in, giving the men suspicious looks, obviously not trusting General Oiseau.

I got to see General Oiseau rueful face one last time as he smiled and Siegfried waved before the woman slammed the door in my face, shutting off my view of the outside world and imprisoning me in the house.

Her name turned out to be Angeline, and she was a very nice woman. When the war ended we went back to my village to see whether any of my relations had come back, yet no one appeared, and I knew neither any names nor addresses, making it difficult for me to track down anyone.

Angeline didn't mind having me, I was a third daughter to her – she had had to elder ones who had moved out, and she doted on me, making sure every one of my needs was met. The village was kind enough to support her financially, yet this was only, as I later found out, because they all thought the Germans had tortured me, or killed my mother, or in some other way acted as villains.

I knew the truth. I knew something I never mentioned to anyone for they wouldn't have believed me. I knew that my Germans had been good, kind and loyal people. I knew the truth.

THE CHIEFY

John Knight

The wind was cold as it blew across the bleak airfield, and the rain drizzled from a darkening sky. We stood under the bombers wing in a forlorn group, eight youngsters out of merry quips. The false laughter of bravado had died away as we suddenly found that we needed to be back in the brightly lit Mess with a manly pint. All the pre flight checks were complete, guns loaded, bomb bay full, everything working. The ground crew were grouped under the other wing probably because we had to make friends with them. Or, were they waiting for us to prove ourselves?

This was our first 'OP'. The very first. We'd trained for months for this moment. Long hours in the classroom, and many hours of flying training followed at long last with 'crewing up'. Eight young, raw, self-conscious strangers off to the Operational Training Unit where together we practised all that we'd been taught. Finally to the Squadron based at this God forsaken spot on the Fens of Lincolnshire. Even then we had two more weeks of practice, and to read up on the mysteries of our aircraft.

Tonight was the real thing. Six aircraft were to bomb a railway depot, and small marshalling yard in Northern France. We'd been heartened at the briefing when the Wing Commander had told us that this one would be, "A piece of cake, chaps." During the next few months we found that he said that every time.

A small Hillman car splashed into the dispersal area, and a head appeared through the passenger window. "Okay, chaps, it's on. Start up at 19.30. You'll get a green from the Control Van. Good Luck."

Slightly embarrassed, we went through the ritual of peeing over the tail wheel before climbing aboard. Again we checked everything over. My charts etc, were as good as I could make them. We plugged in to the intercom and confirmed that we were 'Okay' as the Skipper checked with each one of us.

My belly churned as I heard, and felt, the four engines cough into life. The aircraft lurched as the brakes came off and we started to move. There was no way that we could jump out now! Arriving at the threshold of the runway I almost spewed up when I found that my mind was a complete blank. Looking at my Flight Plan it made no sense. None at all!

The Skipper called to the Engineer, "Brakes off. Full power."

A mighty roar and a great surge of movement we were away careering through darkness. We seemed to rumble along the runway for ever until eventually we were smoothly airborne, and the undercarriage came up with two great thumps as we climbed away.

The intercom clicked. "Confirm the first heading, Nav," the Skipper asked.

I looked at my notes. My voice was thick. "105° magnetic Skip," I croaked. "Cromer in twelve minutes, it's 170° as far as Sheerness."

It gave me great comfort when he asked me to keep him on the ball with headings, and times. A few seconds later, he added, "I'm bloody green as well, you know."

There's not much to tell about that night. We kept on course and height quite well really, and it was a good first trip with just a little light flak. No fighters or searchlights at all. Unlike our later 'OPs' it really was a piece of cake."

But there was something else. Something that was to change the lives of all eight of us. There was an old Ground Crew Flight Sergeant. A 'Chiefy' as they used to be called. He would wander around with his great coat collar turned up, ail soaked forage cap crushed down on his head. Shoulders hunched, hands thrust deep into his pockets he would appear all over the place, especially when there was an 'OP' on and the crew was at the aircraft preparing to go. He would shuffle around the place aimlessly. Our Gunners were all NCO's and although they looked for him in the Sergeants' Mess, he was never there. Strangely, we were the only crew who saw him.

We questioned our Ground Crew Sergeant about him, to be met with a puzzled look.

"Would you say he was old?" he asked. "What does he look like?"

All we could tell him was the old great coat, and oil soaked cap. We had never seen his face.

The Sergeant looked at us oddly. "Always got his hands in his pockets, and slouches like and old man?" he asked.

We confirmed this to him. The Skipper asked, "Well, who is he?"

The Sergeant hesitated, and then drew up to attention, looking at the horizon. "No idea, sir. None at all."

So that was that. We did more trips, and reached twenty. Twenty 'OPs'! We were veterans now, and a bit 'cocky' with it. At least we were cocky on the ground. Up there we were terrified, and it was getting worse with each sortie. Each one seemed worse than the last. On weekends off, or on leave, we were extroverted show offs as we drank and laughed, but with the return to reality we reverted to being very apprehensive young men.

All this time the old 'Chiefy' was still wandering about, visible apparently to only us.

By now we were old hands. There had been commissions, medals, parties, enquiries by the local Constabulary into our behaviour, and much more. I often wonder if the local police ever knew who pushed a milk float into their yard.

It was late August 1944. Our last 'OP' was on the board. A bad one. A very bad one. Daylight to a Norwegian Fiord. A heavily defended enemy Naval Base with a full load. The heaviest we'd ever been, and we definitely did not want to go. Final briefing had been 06.00. The forecasted weather was for 'gin clear continuous'. Both ways! This was a time when a heavy overcast would have been welcome. Also it was one time when we could have done without the 'Wingco' telling us that it would be "A piece of cake, chaps."

We'd had our bacon and eggs, and 'Dinger' Bell our WAAF, driver had taken us to the aircraft. All our checks were done. We were kitted up, and lazing on the grass. The Ground Crew seemed to know how it was, as they polished every single scratch from the windows, and inspected everything twice over. Although we sprawled out like the veterans that in fact we were, we were keyed up, and very nervous indeed.

The chatter had stopped. The Skipper nudged me with his boot making me sit up. He nodded toward the other side of the parking area. The 'Chiefy' was standing there as we'd always seen him, with his oily old cap, and great coat with the collar turned up. He shambled over, and stood looking down at us. This was the first time that we'd actually seen his face, and what a face it was! He looked very old, at least sixty we thought. A weather beaten face, heavily lined, yet with a gentle expression. It was his eyes that surprised me. They were grey-green. One moment sad, the next dancing with amusement. When he spoke, his accent had a soft Welsh lilt.

"So then," he said. "Your last one is it?" He looked up at the morning sky. "See for miles today you can."

The Skipper asked. "Who are you?"

"Don't ask." The 'Chiefy' answered. "I'm everyone, and no one." He looked down at us again, and gave a long sigh. "Old timers are you? This trip will sort you out alright. It's a long flog there, and back. Take my advice, lads, and land back as far north as you can."

I told him we had enough fuel to get back to Base. Anyway, how did he know?

"You're not Aircrew." The Engineer said.

The 'Chiefy' looked at him. "No son, I'm not." If you want me to go away, I will." He looked at each of us. "But I can help you if you'll let me."

"How? How could you help us?" we asked. "How could you possibly do that?"

"I know the 'clangers' you've dropped." He looked at me. "Remember the trip to Hamburg? You gave the course for home slap bang over the target. Very silly." He spoke to the Engineer. "As for you, lad, you tried to cross feed fuel from an empty tank. That was over Rouen wasn't it?" Turning to the Skipper, he eyed him for a moment or so. "And you, Boyo. Remember that night off Cherbourg? You turned starboard instead of port, and you nearly over flew an enemy fighter airfield." He chuckled. "Now there's daft for you."

We were all speechless. Those 'Clangers', and others, should have done for us. But, somehow they hadn't.

He nodded at the Engineer. "No lad, I'm not Aircrew, but I know more about the game than you ever will."

The Skipper asked him, "How do you know all the problems, and mistakes 'Chief'?"

The strange man sat down on the grass. "Take it easy, son. I was with you every time." He plucked a blade of grass and started to chew it. "You should all be dead a few times over, but in my own small way I was able to help." He chewed the grass for a while. "I won't be coming with you this time. This is one you must do on your own."

I looked around. The Ground Crew had disappeared somewhere. It was a fine summer's morning with a cloudless blue sky. Some birds twittered in the hedge behind us, and a tractor chugged away in a nearby field.

It was so very peaceful. We were all silent for a while, each lost in his own thoughts.

Eddy, the Mid Upper Gunner asked him, "Were you really with us, Chiefy? Are you telling us you picked up all our clangers?"

"That I was, and that I did, Boyo." The Chiefy answered.

Someone else spoke. "Okay then, if what you tell us is true, why aren't you going to be with us today?"

Hi answer sounded somehow sad, and the Welsh lilt was more pronounced. "It's the rules, lad. It's the rules."

Although it was all in our minds, this silly fairy story, I felt even more afraid of this coming trip, and wished with all my heart that this scruffy run down old man would come with us. I looked up at him. He was staring at me, his pale eyes seeming to look right inside my head.

His face softened. "Don't be afraid, lad. I can't come with you on your last one. It's the rules you see." He paused and looked at us all. "But there's nothing in the rules that says I can't talk to you."

We moved closer, and formed a semi-circle before him. I can still see it in my mind as we sat cross legged like schoolboys.

He started to talk. "Listen to me, lads. Listen carefully, and remember my words. Take my advice, and act on it. It's all I can do for you now. I have brought you all this far over the last few months, and it's come to the end for us. Soon I shall have another bunch of youngsters to watch over. You'll be on your own."

We moved closer to him. Completely absorbed, we hung on his every word.

"Now then." He began. "You first Skipper. This is the longest trip you'll ever do, and the hardest. Remember your previous mistakes, and learn from them. *Think!* Think not hard, but carefully. Evaluate your every move, there's time enough to do that. You know how the flak floats up at you, how slowly it starts to rise. Well that's your time frame, about five or six seconds, and it's plenty. Don't jerk the controls, it's not a Hollywood film, it's really going to happen. Take avoiding action easily and smoothly. Listen to your Navigator, and watch your heading like a hawk. Listen to your Gunners when they give the 'gen' on flak and fighters. Yours is the easiest job of the lot. Remember lad, fly easy and smooth. Listen to your crew."

'Chiefy' looked at the Gunners. "Three of you. You've been the best of the lot, bar none. Not much I can tell you." He paused for a moment. "Well – maybe you in the rear turret." He looked at Tommy. "Don't muck about on this one, Boyo. You're okay, but keep your mind on the job." He chewed on a fresh blade of grass. "Don't forget you Gunners, deflection first and last. Take your time, and don't rely on pot shots."

We sat quietly, saying nothing. It was uncanny. He seemed to know us inside out.

He carried on. "Wireless Op, you'll do fine." Turning to the Engineer he smiled. "You're alright, lad. Just keep calm, and check everything twice." He shook his head, still smiling. "And this time, try to remember which tank empties first."

I was the last one. It was like waiting to see the Headmaster. I kept thinking of my clanger over Hamburg. Did he really put it right?

"Now you, Boyo. You worry too much! Check each course correction twice. Take your time, but be sure. Don't forget, this trip will be mostly, in fact all of it, will be dead reckoning navigation, so be accurate. Use that drift sight all the time. Check, and double check. Yours is the lead aircraft, so be right."

Then he spoke to us all. "An aeroplane is like a thoroughbred Welsh Collie. Treat it right and it'll look after you. Treat it wrong, and it'll turn round and bite you. Know it. Care for it. It knows what you're thinking, and can sense your fear. It can save you, or kill you.

Make friends with it, touch it gently with affection and it will respond to you. When it gets hurt, as it will today, nurse it tenderly and help it to help you home." He thought for a moment, chewing his grass. "Last of all, *don't panic*. What I'm saying to you is when you're hanging by your fingernails; don't wave your arms about."

We kept silent. Somehow we knew he was right, and that he knew it all.

The 'Chiefy' stood up. His voice was gently. "There lads, I've done my best for you. You fly this one yourselves. It's the rules you know. Don't let me down, Boyo's." He turned, and slouched away. At the far wing tip he stopped and turned. "God bless you, lads," he said. Pushing his oily cap firmly, he went off.

An hour later we turned onto the runway, and took off for our lost 'OP'. It was a bad one for us. Over the target we met the heaviest flak we'd yet encountered. When we turned for home the fighters were on us like angry wasps, but we fought them off after a long running battle. We stayed calm, and did as 'Chief' had told us. The Skipper flew as though he was driving a Rolls Royce. My navigation was spot on, and miracle of miracles, Tommy actually shot one down. The aircraft was badly hit, but we nursed it as the 'Chiefy' had told us. Derek the Engineer had even *talked* to it!

'Chiefy' was right. Our 'Thoroughbred Welsh Collie' had responded, and although sorely hurt, was bringing us safely home.

After many hours we were coming in smoothly, even though we'd lost an engine. The runway was in sigh, and we were nicely lined up with the centre line when the Mid Upper Gunner called, "Look by the control van."

Standing by the chequered van was the 'Chiefy'. His great coat collar up, and that awful cap still crushed down on his head, hands in pockets. We could see him quite clearly as we coasted in.

Softly through our headphones came that now familiar Welsh voice. "Don't look at me! Watch the bloody runway! Remember what I told you, Boyo's. Easy now, lads, you're nearly there. Come on, nice and smooth now."

Our wheels kissed the runway in the smoothest, sweetest landing we'd ever done. That was our last 'OP', and we never saw, or heard of the 'Chiefy' again.

All these years later, I'm still involved with Aviation, and still respect and care for, anything that flies.

Thanks 'Chiefy'. Thanks for everything. May your Welsh valley be forever green.

Mr Beecham's Coat

Cheryl Alleyne

Sidney Pickles placed his cup of tea and newpaper in the space he'd cleared next to the till.

He unfolded the Illustrated London News and scanned the headline. Blimey, what was the world coming to? John Lennon marrying a Japanese woman? That wasn't news, that was –

The door bell tinkled. He looked towards the shop entrance and recognised the hatted silhouette instantly. He straightened himself, adjusted his tie and pulled down the sleeves of his cardigan. Standards. Only way to keep society civilised. If more people thought like him, there wouldn't be –

'Good morning, Mr Pickles.'

'Mrs Beecham.' He dipped his head and smiled at the slight figure. She dipped her head back at him before taking a small step forward. Always the same greeting ritual: but today, she was carrying a much larger bag than usual.

'Now you just stay where you are and let me help.' Sidney sidestepped round the counter, careful not to bump the case of Boer War medals he'd been dusting before the newspaper arrived. He wound his way past the table displays of memorabilia to where the old lady stood. As usual, she was as neat as a pin. He recognised the cotton frock and jacket: it reappeared every spring without fail.

Now he was closer, he peered at her through his bifocals. Only the barest smile tipped her lips and her soft cheeks quivered as though holding the pose was a strain.

He picked up the bulky shopping bag. Goodness knows how she had managed the bus journey and walk to his shop. But, he thought with pride, this lady had standards - and grit - she wouldn't complain. Not like those young ones nowadays –

'Thank you, Mr Pickles, most kind,' said Mrs Beecham. She hesitated as though unwilling to begin what they both knew would be a difficult task. Sidney indicated the way with his hand and she moved slowly to the counter. He positioned himself on the other side and placed the bag between them. She stood ramrod straight but he noted her fingers were shaking in their semblance of prayer.

'This is the last but one,' she said, in no more than a whisper.

He cleared his throat but didn't answer. He undid the zip and when he saw what it contained, looked up at her.

'Are you sure Mrs Beecham?'

She shook her head and, for an instant, he saw her eyes glisten.

'This is what Arthur said I must do. He understands, Mr Pickles, so don't worry.'

Sidney pulled out the single item: an officer's greatcoat. He gave it a quick once over, the least Mrs Beecham would expect him to do. It was in good condition: the grey wool was clean and strong with only the faintest trace of mothballs and tobacco. He unbuttoned the two diagonal rows of brass buttons and opened the coat. Sewn onto the red satin lining was a label bearing the words 'Wilkinsons Sword Co Ltd, Pall Mall'.

'Top price for top quality, I always say.' Sidney said the words with a resigned acceptance as though she'd just put him through the negotiating wringer. Again part of their ritual. And as part of his ritual, he gave silent thanks that she had come into his establishment first and not Reggie Bunce's pawn shop further up the road. That man would cheat his own shadow if he thought he could get away with it.

Sidney handed over the crisp notes. As ever, he felt that he had the best end of the deal. Arthur Beecham had fought for his country and he, Sidney Pickles, was proud to be able to help a brave soldier's wife in her time of need. He recalled the first time she had come into his shop. It was late 1957 and her husband had died in the June heatwave. She had clutched her small bag to her and nervously asked if he would be interested in purchasing a few items.

Over the years with each visit, Mrs Beecham shared a little more of their history. Arthur Beecham had joined the Grenadier Guards in 1914. He had been been invalided home three years later after the third Ypres offensive. But the man who returned was a shadow of the man he'd been, and her husband became the only child that his twenty-two year old wife would ever have. Sidney had bought an impressive array of his medals – Military Cross, First and second bars, Distinguished Cross, Distinguished Service Order as well as all the campaign ones. A true hero who Sidney would have loved to meet. Though from what Mrs Beecham had told him, there wouldn't have been any stirring tales of derring-do: for the rest of his life, Arthur Beecham refused to say a word about the war.

That day, Mrs Beecham did she as she always did and visited the items she'd previously sold him. She picked each one up and spoke to it in a low soothing tone as though comforting a child. Of course, if anyone asked Sidney about one of her treasures, he simply said someone had already bought it and directed them to something similar.

The next morning, Sidney shuffled down stairs to open up. He switched on the light and almost fainted. A mannequin wearing Arthur Beecham's coat was blocking his way. How on earth did that get there? He was sure he'd left the garment in the store room when Mrs Beecham had gone. Maybe he'd got more done yesterday than he'd remembered? He tutted. His bloody memory must be playing tricks again. Still, the coat did look good on the wooden figure with its handsome painted face and Kitchener–like waxed moustache. He would dress it up properly when he had the chance. But not today: he had a list as long as his arm to do first. He manoeuvred the dummy next to a helmet display and, after collecting his stocktake sheet and pen, made his way to the cabinet full of cloth and metal insignias.

Mrs Beecham came in early. Sidney was surprised since she usually only visited once a fortnight. He met her halfway just as she caught sight of the mannequin wearing her husband's coat. A flicker of panic crossed her face.

'Is everything alright, Mrs Beecham?'

'Is that where you're going to keep Arthur?' she asked.

Sidney hesitated, wondering as to the correct response.

'The helmets, Mr Pickles.' Her lips made a little moue and she lowered her voice. 'They're all German… Arthur wouldn't be comfortable there…'

He felt himself blush. Stupid blighter. How could he have been so insensitive? He quickly assured her it was only temporary, and for good measure shifted the mannequin a few feet away from the offending headwear. A smile replaced Mrs Beecham's pucker.

Relieved, Sidney went back to the cabinet he'd been working on and resumed his counting. Every now and then, out of the corner of his eye, he saw her stroke the woollen sleeve of her husband's coat. Her lips never ceased moving. Sidney thought that, even with his burns and disfigurement, Arthur Beecham had been a lucky man. He had had a lifetime − and more − of his wife's devotion. Not many could say the same what with that women's lib tosh and the like.

Although the next day was Sunday, his one day off, Sidney went down to the shop and continued stocktaking. It was only when he moved in the direction of the German helmets that he noticed the mannequin wearing Mr Beecham's coat was missing. He looked all around but couldn't spot the familiar figure. Had he shifted it after Mrs Beecham's departure? Bloody hell, if he had he must be losing his memory. He thought back through what he'd done the previous day but no recollection of moving the dummy surfaced.

He walked to the front of the shop and checked for any sign of the errant mannequin. It was only when he entered the side room that he found it: next to the photograph cabinet showing campaigns of the first world war. Sidney scratched his head. He decided to leave it where it was and for good measure, made a note of this fact on his sheet. He then spent the rest of the day completing the stocktake.

The following morning, Sidney went straight to the side room. No sign of Mr Beecham's coat. He shook his head. What was going on? Maybe he did need to see the doctor. He checked his record but then wondered if he'd forgotten to write down his later actions. He eventually found the mannequin alongside a shelf of military headwear. He picked up the nearest cap and looked at the tag. It listed Captain Arthur Beecham as its owner.

Over the next couple of months, Sidney found the mannequin

either close to something that had belonged to Arthur Beecham or in the middle of one of the British or Allied displays. He found this a surprising source of comfort and decided it was best not to think too deeply about it. Mrs Beecham never once questioned this constant relocation. But it gave Sidney an idea.

After a final polish, Sidney stood back to admire the mannequin. Not only was it wearing Arthur Beecham's greatcoat and officer's cap, but many of the items brought in by Mrs Beecham. The rows of medals on the chest now gleamed as did the boots and gaiters.

He moved the mannequin so it was under a spotlight at the front of the shop – pride of place – to be seen by all who entered Pickles Militaria Ltd.

'That looks wonderful.'

Sidney had paid no attention to the jingle of the opening door but now he turned. He straightened himself and tipped his head to Mrs Beecham. Today, in the heat, no jacket accompanied her favourite frock.

'Do you think Mr Beecham is pleased?' he asked, with a smile.

Mrs Beecham nodded. Her eyes twinkled at him. 'Very.'

After sharing their wonderment at Neil Armstrong's first steps on the moon, Sidney left her admiring the display.

Summer changed to autumn and autumn took on a darker hue. Mrs Beecham visited every day except Sunday. To make up for this, she stayed twice as long on a Monday. Sidney enjoyed her company and made sure that even if he was very busy he spent some time with her. Mr Beecham, despite his prime position, continued to move around the shop each night, and every morning Sidney would hunt for him – on several occasions he was even found on the first floor where the model collections were kept. And just as Mrs Beecham held conversations with her husband, so too did Sidney.

December segued into early January, and Mrs Beecham's visits became progressively fewer. Every two days, then every three. The next time she came in, Sidney invited her for a cup of tea. As she held out her hand to take some sugar, he noticed how thin her wrists had become. He went straight up to his kitchen and returned with a plate of biscuits. She ate four and, he thought, if it wasn't for her standards, she probably would have eaten more.

'Is everything alright, Mrs Beecham?' he ventured.

'Yes, thank you, Mr Pickles. Now I must go and tell dear Arthur who I met on the bus. He'll be most surprised.' She rose slowly from her seat. 'Thank you very much for the tea, Mr Pickles, I do appreciate your kindness.'

Sidney nodded and the next morning when he found Mr Beecham beside the kettle and his biscuit tin, he took the hint. Whenever Mrs Beecham came to the shop, he served her tea and always with plenty of biscuits.

The February weather took a turn for the worse but still Mrs Beecham battled the elements and made her thrice weekly visits. True British stamina, he thought. You had to hand it to the old girl, she might look frail but there must be steel within those bones. Good on her. On her next visit, he gave her some fruit cake he'd bought and warned her that - as he had done every year – he would be closing the shop for a fortnight. For his 'holiday' when he would take day trips to purchase more stock and see what the competition was up to.

But on the day of his first outing, Sidney came downstairs early to find Mr Beecham – or rather the mannequin – blocking his path. He almost chuckled as he remembered his initial shock at these occurrences when he noticed that Mr Beecham was missing his coat. Was this the start of a new game? He had a few minutes to spare so he set off, imagining he'd find it after his usual hunt. But that was not to be. He searched high and low – including the German displays which Mr Beecham normally steered clear of.

Sidney racked his brains as to where the coat might be. He checked the front door: it was still locked and all the windows were intact. He even went back upstairs and searched his flat. Worrying thoughts of early dementia surfaced, but he knew that there was no way on this earth he would have let the coat leave his shop. It was Mrs Beecham's prized possession, one that he was temporarily responsible for. He hadn't – he just couldn't have – let her down. His standards wouldn't allow it. He didn't make it to Ramsgate that day. After thoroughly searching his premises, he temporarily moved the dummy to the storeroom.

The next morning, he was surprised to find it still there. The mannequin hadn't moved. For the next few days, it stayed in the backroom still without its coat. Sidney made a few trips out but his heart wasn't in it. He wasn't expecting Mrs Beecham for almost a fortnight, but he found himself trying to think up possible explanations for when she did arrive. And any chance he got, he searched some more.

It was during Sidney's first morning of his reopening that he thought he'd found a way to solve the problem. He would purchase another greatcoat. Surely with his contacts, he could find one which would – he gulped at this point – make Mrs Beecham believe it was her husband's. It wasn't the ideal solution, but he couldn't bear the thought of...

Sidney broke off when he heard someone enter the shop. He looked up to see the local constable making his way towards him. He squinted. What the...?

PC Hobbs greeted him and removed a bulky woollen coat from under his arm. He placed it on the counter.

'Does this belong to you?' asked PC Hobbs.

Sidney picked it up just to make sure. He confirmed it did and mentioned it had gone missing from his shop.

PC Hobbs wore a puzzled expression. 'Are you sure you didn't sell it?'

'Of course I'm sure. I know my own stock. Why? Where did you find it? Who had it?'

'Mrs Rose Beecham.'

It was Sidney's turn to look puzzled. Had he given it to her? But why would he do that? No, he was positive he hadn't...

'Did she buy much from you? Maybe you forgot you'd sold it to her?' The constable's voice tailed off.

Sidney bristled at the man and briefly explained his purchases from her. 'And tell me, Constable,' he tried to think of the most outlandish thing possible, ' were you arresting her when you discovered this contraband?'

PC Hobbs raised his bushy eyebrows. 'No, Mr Pickles. A

neighbour had reported not seeing Mrs Beecham for about a fortnight. We broke into her flat.'

Sidney frowned. 'Is she alright?'

'No, she's not, Mr Pickles. She'd fallen on the kitchen floor and hadn't been able to get up.' He paused. 'I'm sorry to tell you but that's where she died. Hypothermia by the looks of it. But when we found the body, this overcoat was tucked around her.'

Sidney saw the questions in the constable's eyes.

'I'm not sure what's going on but you might need to check the rest of your stock…'

PC Hobbs reached into his pocket. He took out a Pickles Militaria tag and another item. He handed them to him.

Sidney gasped. He placed the tag on the counter and with his fingertips felt the weight and shape of the remaining object.

A lump rose in his throat as he gazed at the Victoria Cross in his hand. The door bell tinkled. Both he and PC Hobbs looked up.

But no one was there.

Navex RBS
(Navigation Exercise Radar Bombing System)

Geoff Faragher

Having transferred fuel from one wing tank to another to bring the Vulcan aircraft's centre of gravity within the required tolerance, I set the calculator aside and relaxed. The soft lights from the instrument panel reflected onto the cabin windows and little could be seen of the darkened sky beyond, although an arc of faded sunlight was just about visible along the earth's horizon, well below us. Our sortie profile was nominated as a navigation exercise (Navex) and it terminated with a simulated nuclear attack on a previously specified target within Liverpool's urban sprawl using the radar bombing system (RBS).

It was warm in the aircraft's cabin, and I glanced idly at the outside temperature gauge – minus 70 degrees! Ouch, this was not the night to have to abandon the aircraft! Training had suggested that once the ejector seat had thrust its occupant clear of the aircraft, it would free-fall to about 10,000 feet before tipping out its passenger and deploying the parachute. Just imagine free-falling from our cruising height of 45,000 feet having first suffered the trauma and shock that necessitated you to eject in the first place. The prospect of exposure to the bitter ambient temperatures alone was more than enough to switch my mind to consider other things.

I needlessly scanned the instrument panel in an attempt to prevent my mind dwelling on the scary side of flying. The auto-pilot was set on a heading of 330 degrees, we continued to fly at 45,000 feet; the speed registered at 0.89 indicated mach and the control surfaces indicators and the artificial horizon meter confirmed that were in level flight. The compass bearing hadn't varied in over twenty five minutes and showed that we continued to head towards Iceland, having left RAF Waddington in Lincolnshire earlier that evening. The Skipper had control, and as the co-pilot I had time to allow my mind to wander.

Iceland was not our destination that night. After travelling 1000 kilometres in a northerly direction our flight plan was to turn sharply south and head back towards Liverpool. Mark Hacker, our Navigator Plotter was testing his skills at navigation assuming that the aircraft's automatic positioning avionics were not available to him. He sat with his maps alongside the two other rear crew members on the lower deck. Whereas the two pilots occupied eject seats on the raised upper deck, the rear crew members sat in-line facing rearwards on static seats. On the starboard side was the Navigator Radar, Tim Clarke, who wouldn't be doing much on this trip until we undertook a simulated bombing attack on the city of Liverpool; our last activity before returning to base at RAF Waddington. On the port side sat John Dean, the Air Electronics Officer; John would be monitoring the aircraft's electrical systems and reporting our position back to Bomber Command Operations Centre every fifteen minutes; but again, we were not in hostile territory and so he would not be operating the aircraft's electronic counter measures. Mark Hacker was the only crew member totally preoccupied trying to determine precisely where we were using his basic dead-reckoning skills; that's pencilled track-lines on maps, rulers, protractors, wrist watch and all that. It was a necessary part of his annual qualification as a V-Bomber navigator. There would be other sorties when the specialist skills of the other crew members would be tested, but tonight it was exclusively the Nav Plotter's show.

Without warning the four fire warning lights illuminated, bright red; all four engines were on fire! Or so it seemed! They immediately went out! Because of the relative darkness, those red lights were bright enough to light up the whole cabin.

Having overcome my shock, I glanced across to the Skipper, whose eyes had practically popped-out of their sockets. His hand hovering near the fire warning display panel; his forefinger extended ready to press the button lights and fire off the engine extinguishers.

We looked at each other in disbelief. In my experience so far, engine fires only occur on the flight simulator, they don't happen half-way to Iceland, over the cold North Atlantic Sea, at 45,000 feet with an outside temperature at minus 70 degrees. And then the four engine fire lights illuminated again!

This didn't make sense.

I turned and looked rearwards to find that Mark (the clumsy) Hacker had left his seat and the other two showed no sign of the expected panic!

'Mark,' called the Captain over the intercom. 'Where are you?'

'I'm taking a star shot using the sextant, Skipper. Did you need something?'

'Yes! I need you to take your bloody elbow off the fire warning light test button!'

Just One Big Game

Steve Morris

"Just look at the state of him. Good grief. What were you thinking of? This is serious, you fool."

"I'm telling you he is the best!" I replied.

We both watched Hayden in the mess. Seemingly oblivious to us, he sat as always in this same position, at the same table ritualistically arranging the food around his plate into some sort of personal symmetry while slowly nodding his head inside his headphones. I wasn't sure if he could hear the Commander. If he was, he could probably recall and repeat each and every word of our conversation. Backwards if he wants to.

The Commander shook his head.

"Just tell me where the hell you found him again? I've heard you took him out of some bloody care home. I've heard you tried to recruit a whole bunch of 'em. Oxford not good enough for military intelligence recruitment these days? Do you know what we are up against? So let me get this right, this guy," – he couldn't even bring himself to say his name – "is heading our first strike team? That's just bloody brilliant, that is!"

I was not happy with this view, even from a senior officer.

"With all due respect, Commander, he's a bloody genius and makes some of your recent Oxbridge recruits look remedial. We've never seen a mind like his."

"Well, Hayden's a damned freak if you ask me. We've had it now!"

After that the commander slammed the mess door as he stormed through it.

"We've had it now!" I heard him shout again as he slammed another door further down the corridor.

All hell was brewing. It had been bubbling under for some time.

The war was about to begin any day. We were all involved in the final preparations.

However, the next war was to be very different to any other

previous wars.

It would begin on the Internet.

Hayden had been selected due to his downright prodigious mathematical talents. You just don't learn skills like those in any university. That was something you were born with. He was simply one in a billion and I am glad he was on our side.

The way that the seemingly otherwise clumsy and untidy Hayden used mathematics was both as beautiful and as cold as the Chopin melodies he was obsessed with. However, he saw none of its beauty. I can't imagine that Hayden had ever found anything 'beautiful'.

Hayden had been recruited and trained for a specific pre-emptive strike to bring down the entire electronic communications structure in the East, prior to an invasion. He was an unlikely candidate to kick off what would be one of the biggest fights in world history.

Warfare had moved on from its primitive history of trenches and tanks.

We all had become increasingly reliant on the Internet for our everyday lives. We had become far too reliant on it for our own good. I often considered what actual part of our lives we couldn't actually live via the Internet. It seemed that people all over the world no longer needed to leave their homes to perform everyday activities. It just wasn't natural. But then why did we have any further need to hit each other with clubs?

In terms of warfare: bringing down a country's Internet network would bring down their entire infrastructure. If done in the proper order, a country's social, industrial, commercial and military communications networks could be incapacitated to make them ripe for invasion before they even knew what was happening.

I sat down by Hayden, that night before the war. It was just any other night of the week to him, spent on the same table with the same choice of meal. His team's job was to electronically cripple the very data structure that held the Easter bloc countries together, prior to formalities of 'land and air operations' which would cause minimum casualties.

It was hard to believe that it could be a 'last supper'.

Talking to the autistic Hayden was never easy at the best of times. His eyes would lock on you for a quarter of a second if you were lucky, then they would just dart around rapidly from left to right. My eyes could never keep up with their speed. His sole effort at being polite was one of his split-second artificially forced smiles on one side, almost like a wink that returned his face to its original concentrated expression before you had actually realised what those wrinkles by his mouth were there for.

He explained to me what he had achieved during that day, what music he would be transcribing tonight and what computer games he would be playing after, each in their strictly allocated time slot. He didn't listen to my questions, but would stockpile them to answer later, in their correct order, after he had finished his statement. He had everything organised for the next day. Hayden knew how to hack the security algorithms to cause the blackout. I often urged him to share his strategies with his fellow 'troops' in case he ever 'caught the flu'. He did try but wasn't good at explaining his techniques. He had a massive amount of responsibility on his shoulders and was blissfully unaware of it.

Only a person like Hayden could not think about the next day and what it would entail. To say he was focussed on his current task was an understatement. His current task was supper. Attempting to change the subject of the conversation away from Hayden's one-way monotonic monologue was rather pointless. As to any algorithms needed to crack the code, that wasn't a problem, as I knew he could do in the background with his eyes shut, probably while he found something else to keep his mind busy.

There was no one on earth who could hack and crack codes like he could. Basic military training we forgot, as Hayden had his own discipline, trapped in his own bizarre rituals of his own bizarre world. He had enough trouble just walking around stores in town to follow any regular "parade ground" military training. That was how he was and we were not going to change that. And it would be Hayden who would open the door for the beginning of World War III. For a moment, he was to be the most powerful man on Earth perhaps. We were relying on this young man sat with his headphones on in front of his strategically symmetrical supper to simultaneously close down all phone lines, mobile communications, satellite communications and radio signals of an entire continent. Thirty minutes after his morning's work, thousands of tanks would cross a border in the hope of meeting very little resistance.

I needed recruits who were fit for this modern conflict. By that I meant digital-age, digitally minded assassins who were as cold, numerical, and unemotional as the very machines they spent their lives sitting in front of.

I needed brilliantly minded soldiers without remorse, guilt, feelings, and vulnerabilities and who could program computers in their sleep. I needed robots really. So I got out there searching.

Previously we had been selecting and training the very best of Oxbridge mathematicians as was our traditional 'Milk-round' headhunting ground. Some of these were excellent, but they had to also work at their mathematics. They needed effort and rest. They had vulnerabilities. What I needed were recruits who were naturally born with the very brilliance they would need to play against the world's best mathematical tacticians without any strain whatsoever, as if it were all just one leisure activity.

So I tracked down a careful selection of highly autistic young mathematicians. Looking back in history it would seem likely now that the most successful of our brilliantly creative talents in the fields of music, literature, design and invention all seemed to exhibit autistic traits. They needed an outlet in which to blossom, otherwise their skills would remain wasted in their unfulfilling lives. What better use for their prodigious maths talents than electronic warfare?

What I ended up with were a crew of highly individually gifted, talented, incredibly misunderstood recruits with previously unrealised and untapped logical talents. I nurtured them. I changed them into soldiers, of a kind. However their social and communication skills were lacking somewhat and they did not work well as a team. There was no way that they could adjust to military life so we had to move to accommodate them. This did not go down well with many of our personnel. However times had moved on. We would be fighting in a different world in a different time and I needed a different type of soldier. The Commander would have to realise this. I am sure that our enemies were fully aware of it.

Satellite observations deemed the time to be exactly right.

Our military were in place. The time had come for the black-out.

"5... 4... 3... 2... 1... Okay, Hayden turn 'em off," smiled the Commander.

Nothing.

"Okay. Off they go. Execute"

Nothing.

"Execute. Damn you."

"Execute. Execute. Execute"

Nothing.

The room looked at the young genius.

"I can't do that as Scream21 has been put in charge of their security. Scream21 is defending their security in their command centre"

"What do you mean? Who the hell is Scream Sodding 21?"

"Scream21 is defending their security. I can't let you bomb him because we will play chess again tomorrow night and he is 3-1 up."

Every one else avoided the Commander's gaze blankly.

Enraged, he stamped around the centre screaming, "Anyone else here know the code? Anyone know how to execute?"

No one did.

POST-WAR LOVE

Heidi Vella

George looked out through the window of the dining room at the rain that poured relentlessly. He sat with his arms rested on the table next to the carefully laid out cutlery. Every other minute Georges twitch knocked the cutlery together making a clanging sound.

Dianne walked in holding two plates filled with beef stew. She placed a plate in front of George and one in the place set opposite him. George looked blankly down at the food, though he were looking into a black hole. He began to eat absentmindedly.

Dianne took a deep breath, pushed her short bobbed dark hair behind her ears and sat at the table. She watched her husband eat like the food tasted of nothing and her throat began to swell, and her heart felt heavy again. This was a regular feeling for Dianne now, the wife of an officer returned from a long gruelling war, The Great War. She had waited and prayed everyday that her husband would return alive; that was all she wanted. She worked hard in the factory to help the war effort, she wrote to her husband every day hoping that her letter would give him strength. She always thought that as long as he came home, no mater in what state, with missing limbs, scars; it wouldn't faze her, because she would have her husband back and the war would be over.

Instead, after the armistice the reality of war had left a putrid taste in the mouth and a pain in the chest like no other. There was no triumphant return for George, the man she adored. He came home a shell, his memory lost, with a disturbing twitch and his mind gone to the unknown. He had forgotten the whole of their married life. He remembered meeting and falling in love with Dianne, but not that they had married and been happily married for ten years. He knew he loved her deeply and that if he were better he would marry her again tomorrow. It was upsetting for George to have lost a whole chunk of his life, though his mind was so fuzzy, his thoughts so jarred, he tried to think of nothing at all. It was to much, to remember, to remember what had passed in the last four years.

Dianne watched him mess the table as his hand twitched trying to pick up stew with his fork. It seemed so undignified that a man who had led men in war was reduced to a squirming, aged, frail being who struggled to eat without making a mess like a baby.

He looked up disappointedly.

"Sorry," he muttered.

She smiled through her pain, lent forward and touched his hand. "Its fine darling, please don't worry. I will clean it when you have finished."

He looked at her sincerely with heavy eyes. "Thank you."

She wondered what he must think of her now. She is not the beauty of ten years ago, she knows that. Maybe on his release he thought he would be coming home to a young beautiful woman. She began to feel like a disappointment. She is not the woman she used to be. She has gained lines and a little weight around the hips and stomach, and she has lost her spark, a little, she thought. Once she could make any body feel like the luckiest person in the room; now she couldn't even make her husband feel better or happy that war is over and he made it home alive, to her.

She pushed her food around her plate and ate as much as she could manage so as not to upset him, and to encourage him to eat as well.

They finished eating, their plates still half full, and left the modest dinning room to retire in the sitting room.

The sitting room was adequate enough, cosy, with a fire place to warm them in the winter, though not as light an airy as the dinning room was in summer, so Dianne opened a small window as the rain had ceased. George sat down in an old wooden rocking chair that his grandfather had given to him as a present before he moved in with Dianne. He loved the chair, it was one of the few objects around him he knew and remembered well. He found it comforting to gently rock the night away looking out onto the pebbled London Street. Sometimes he would fall asleep in the chair while Dianne watched him. She would go up close to him and look at all the new lines and creases in his face up close. Touch his brittle lips gently with her soft hands, rub his stubble and stroke his hair; it was the only time she felt she could really touch him without him seeming like he would break or, she was intruding on his person. She had refrained from doing it recently though as the last time, he had woke abruptly, eyes wide like a cat and bolted forwards suddenly; he nearly knocked her out. She was accustomed to him waking like this - in a frenzy almost, but he had never done so before while she was touching him; she always thought her caress subconsciously soothed him.

George sat in the chair gently rocking looking out the window. "Would you like the wireless on?"

He moved his eyes slowly to hers. "No, this is fine."

She smiled, he moved his stare back to the outside world. She continued to look at him, moved her lips to speak but couldn't, and, even if she could, she didn't know what to say.

She walked away, though didn't know to where. She felt restless and frustrated, like she wanted to scream and shake him. She sat down in a chair and put her head in her hands.

Just then the doorbell rang. Dianne feared it was his mother. That was the last thing she needed; his mother was always so fussy, fussing around him and ordering Dianne about. She was so proud when her little boy went to war, while he was away she would waltz round the neighbourhood telling stories about her son at war; like no one else's son was at war. She would tell stories about George in the local shops that Dianne thought she had never heard before and was convinced she must of made them up. Maybe she was just being harsh, we all have our ways of coping, she thought.

George looked round from his chair with a nervous expression on his face. Maybe he was thinking the same thing as her, she thought.

"I will take a look and see who it is."

She opened the door and was greeted by George's younger brother Luke, holding his hat with a cautious smile on his face.

Dianne breathed a sigh of relief. "Hello Luke. Come in, how are you?"

Luke stepped in and hung up his hat and coat.

"Can't complain. You?"

"Yes, fine thank you."

"So, how's old George?"

Dianne tried to compose herself but the welcome relief of a friend took over her. She covered her face with her hands. George put his arm round her and gave her a strong hug.

"Not good, eh? Don't worry, De, he will be fine, he just needs some more time. And lots of that love you give him!" He gently rubbed her back, then pulled her delicately away.

"Now, dry those tears missy and let me go and see what I can do for that brother of mine."

Dianne wiped her tears with her hanky while Luke bounced into the sitting room. Dianne wished George had been like Luke during the war, not so hasty to go to the battlefield. Luke had served only a short time in the trenches, as soon as he received a small injury a friend of his arranged for him to have an office job translating and breaking codes. Luke had offered George the same; but he didn't think it such an honourable thing to leave your men. Dianne never agreed – every individuals war effort was as important as the next – why was it more important to send young men; sons, fathers, and brothers to their deaths and follow them? All those fine men slaughtered just like that. Maybe that's what is haunting him so much now, it would haunt me too, she thought.

She could still remember the day when George signed up for the war. Dianne had begged George to take her to the Palace that night as there was a show she wanted to see. George, as always, indulged his wife happily and off they went. Except that night what Dianne hadn't realised was, also going to be there was recruiting Army officers. They had laid out tables and were asking for men to sign up. At first Dianne didn't think much about it; until a beautiful woman in a red and blue dress came on stage smiling and walking around all the tables on stage. She began to belt out *Rule Britannia* and when she had finished she sauntered off stage and walked all through the aisles up and down touching men on the arms and shoulders, asking them to follow her. As she came by George she stroked his head and gave a huge sultry smile. Dianne was astounded when George got up and started following her also, before she had a chance to say a word. He signed up that night and Dianne's heart sank right there and then. When they got home they had a massive row and somehow in her fit of despair she broke a little trinket he had given her when they met, that had one big butterfly painted on the top, she had kept her little collection of semi-precious stones in it. It smashed into three pieces, well that was it for Dianne and she went to bed in tears. She was angry, upset, but most of all scared of loosing him. The next morning he presented the trinket to her all fixed, somehow he had managed to put it back together again – you could still see the lines where it had been fixed but it was whole again.

George said to her: "I don't want to leave you either darling, but, the war needs men and so us men must go."

She smiled at him resolutely and kissed his smooth cheek,. "Yes, I know. I am just scared of loosing you, I wouldn't know what to do."

"Don't be silly, my angel. I will be home before you know it."

Dianne never did believe him when he said that and she was right not to; it was three and a half years before he came back for good.

Dianne checked her face in the little antique mirror that hung in the hall. At least he kept his promise in someway, she thought, before walking into the sitting room.

Luke was sitting next to George telling him about his new promotion he had just received. Dianne could tell he had lost the upbeat tone in his voice that he had walked in with. Luke had always looked up to his brother, he knew everyone was proudest of him, and he was too. George was always good to him, every time he came round he sort of expected a miracle to of happened. He always envisaged George slapping him on the back and them having a couple of whiskey's and a chat. It never was like that though for the last ten months it has been the same, very little improvement. He shook less maybe, but his mind was always somewhere outside the room; with all the other lost souls Luke always thought. Their mother had wanted him to have shock treatment after this snide doctor befriended her and convinced her it would be the only way to cure him; as long as she parted with a handsome sum of money of course. Dianne had flatly refused and so had Luke.

The evening past as pleasantly as possible, the dark drew in and the draft chilled the room. Mostly there was silence in-between Lukes chattering about his job, gossip he heard or his hope for the future. Dianne liked to listen to him; it was so quiet after the war, he filled the air with comforting noise, the notion that there was some normality left.

George thanked his brother for coming and excused himself for bed.

"Shall I help you darling?" Dianne asked.

"No. Thank you, dear," he replied.

Dianne smiled at the use of 'dear'.

George walked to the room; he had been sleeping in the spare room since his return, somehow it didn't seem right to lie side by side.

He sat on the bed and blinked angrily. He felt anger at his life now, the pain he knew he caused his wife, all the dead men and boys he saw blown apart before him. Limbs flying, intestines slithering, a smile on a hopeful face then that same face with a whole on one side. How did it all fit together? What were you supposed to do after this? It was easier not to feel or think, but deep down he wanted the numbness to go away, to love again, to love for all those who now couldn't. It just wasn't that easy. He picked up one of the pictures Dianne had left on the bed stand for him to look at, in the vain hope it might help recover something of her pre-war husband. He looked at the picture; Dianne smiling, him to, handsome with full lips and large eyes, Dianne wearing a cute hat, her hair longer then and let loose. They were on a beach somewhere, he didn't know where, but they looked happy. George stroked Dianne's hair in the picture with his finger then put it below his pillow.

Dianne and Luke sat in the lounge together.

"Will you pour me a brandy, Luke, please?" Dianne asked.

Luke poured her the drink and sat by her side.

"He is getting better all the time, De. He is not lost to us I can see that," Luke said rubbing her shoulder.

Dianne sipped her brandy and enjoyed the warmth that passed through her as a much needed comfort.

"I hope so Luke, I really do."

Luke squeezed her hand. "Well I better be off, unless you need to talk? I can always stay for a while if you need me to."

Dianne shook her head, "I think you need a rest from talking, do you not?" she said teasingly.

"Don't be cheeky, Miss De Goodnight. I will see you soon."

Dianne went to get up, "No, I can let myself out, don't get up."

Dianne smiled, "Thank you, and goodnight."

"Goodnight, De."

As the door closed she poured herself another drink. She went to the drawing board and pulled open the second draw. In it was the trinket that George had fixed; she picked it up and examined all it's cracked. She ran her fingers over each crack, opened the trinket and inside was a small locket she had forgotten she had put there. Inside the locket was a picture of George as a child; it had been his grandmothers and she left it to him when she died. Dianne put the locket on the side and sat down in the rocking chair. The chair was still warm from George. She put the trinket in her lap.

She began to think what was left for her in life now; she had hoped for new beginnings after the war, maybe a baby for her them to love and raise. That all seemed impossible now, unreachable. She felt that in her heart she had written George off and that upset her the most. She never could have imagined she could feel this way; but it was so hard, did he even love her? She thought about this for a while. She knew it would be easier maybe if she believed he was beyond help or he didn't love her at all because then she could move on instead of passing the days in limbo. She picked up the trinket and admired the cracks; it was whole despite being full of cracks – a bit like George, she thought. She loved her trinket just as much with cracks, couldn't she do the same with her husband…? Yes she could, and she would put him back together like he put back the trinket, he will never be the same, like the trinket isn't, but he will be hers and he will come back to her one day. Dianne placed the trinket on the table near the rocking chair and put the locket with George's picture on the chain round her neck. She looked at the empty room, tided it quickly and went to bed.

Dianne woke early that morning and the sun was beaming outside. She walked round and opened all the windows and breathed in the air, though London air it maybe. She made his favourite breakfast of poached eggs and ham. When she heard George come down from his room she took a deep breath. As he walked into the kitchen she greeted him with a kiss on the cheek, he was a little surprised but he didn't flinch.

"I made you your favourite breakfast – poached eggs and ham, the toast is just coming."

"Thank you."

He sat down at his place on the table. Dianne brought in the toast. George looked up from his food at his wife.

"I do love you. You know that, don't you?"

Dianne melted inside, relief rushed through her bones, and her legs turned to jelly. Tears streamed down her face.

"Yes, George. I know."

WAR LAND

I thought I'd give a quick synopsis of the story, as some details are unclear, though that is deliberate. It is set in an unnamed war, completely fictional. It is pre-arms, I was going for a seventh century affect, and it plays out in about a fifteen minute period of time.

Nyla

> For a million men may fall,
> And the world can remain,
> But the smallest of wars,
> The whole world can change.

Sayid clambered nervously over the trench wall. He had been trained and tutored in the art of war, taught the principles of survival, but it wasn't hypothetical anymore. It was real. His friends and comrades were lined up on both sides of him, staring their fate square in the face. The frontline appeared to stretch for miles, and the enemy borders lined the horizon, the sun rising slowly from where the enemy were preparing. The sky was a blood red mist, hanging low over the men's heads, taunting them. Two trees, leafless and lifeless stood just metres apart in the middle of no-man's land. They roughly marked where the two conflicting armies met, where men from both sides fell mercilessly at the strikes of their enemy. The ground was a matted maroon, broken soil mixed with rivers of dark red blood.

It was an unforgiving time, pre adolescent boys forced into the folds of war, fighting for their lives, for a freedom they would never experience. Sayid was just one of thousands to tread upon the frontline, just another number that would, at some point, be referred to in the future as a tragic loss in the history of this land. He knew all too well that the only reason he was on this team was because of where he happened to have been born. His fate had been aligned for him as he grew, a tiny embryo in the depths of his mother's womb.

Each and every man stood tensely on their border, awaiting

the screech of the whistle that would inform them it was time to attack, time to defend. The desolate land stretched out far in front of them, taunting them. It would eventually destroy them, steal their lives away, and set them free. If any man survived this attack they would be front runner in the next. Sometimes, for Sayid, it seemed that it would be better for him, for them all, if the earth swallowed them up, rescued them from the torture of war.

The boy on the right of Sayid trembled, he was what was referred to as a 'twitcher'. Every soldier was nervous of course, it was only natural, but twitchers were the worst of all. They sat in their bunks, rocking backwards and forwards, often ranting of family they had waiting for them in their homes. Sayid had seen this boy several times, crying in his bunk, constantly screaming for his mother, he was, after all, still no more than a child. It was not an unusual sight to see a boy soldier beaten by the sights, sounds and smells of war, but this particular boy seemed much so sadder than the others. Sayid thought he had heard the officers call him Salim. Sayid remembered his grandmother teaching him names and their meanings when he was just a boy. Salim, she had told him, meant sane, unimpaired. That did not seem to reflect upon the personality of this young twitcher. He was terrified, his fear held him back from his duties. He barely looked thirteen. Still a young boy, he was from a small village where most of the inhabitants were family. He was clearly petrified of what loomed ahead of him. Then there were the 'hardy' soldiers, they were predominantly the men and boys who had no one waiting for them on the other side of the war. They had lost all their loved ones well before the war and were somewhat loveless. They fought for the sake of fighting and nothing more. War ripped the souls out of every man enrolled in the force. It ripped out their souls and crushed them beneath its heavy foot, one by one, but the hardy soldiers had already lost their souls.

The whistle screamed at them to run, it was their time to follow those who had gone before them, they had to follow suit, just as every other boy and man had done in the weeks and months prior to the moment they had to put their mortality to the test. For two epic long seconds every man stood still, paralyzed. It was a moment of sheer terror, there was not a man who was not afraid, not even the hardy soldiers could withstand the horror that their hearts succumbed to. Beating rapidly and rhythmically, the men took their first step forward, in complete unison. The cavalry came from behind and rode off in front, spears held stealthily in the right hands of the seated soldiers. Horses of black, white and brown hurtled forwards as they came into contact with the horses of the opposing army. Spears struck those of the enemy, metal on metal, as the horsemen collided, clashing, battling, wrestling for whatever freedom they could lay their hands on. But no matter how hard they fought, freedom was something that neither army could achieve for themselves, freedom was for those who already had their freedom in place.

The foot soldiers marched forwards, some ran, some staggered behind, attempting to get lost in the confusion, running backwards, back into the trenches of their own men, where it was safe. They were only a few miles from their loved ones, but the closer they were to death, the further they were from home. Sayid knew this, Sayid had known from the moment he left, he would not make it back those few miles to home. He wished if he could only flee the war, he would be even nearer to his home, he could build a new home if he wished, he could go anywhere, do anything. But where he was, scurrying through no-man's land, heavy metal weighing down his entire body, he was trapped in the evil cycle of war. The only escape he had was to keep moving forwards, steadily approaching the enemy lines.

Sayid saw Salim, still to his right, lagging behind him slightly. He was in no hurry. Salim still had dreams of being reunited with his family, Sayid had given up hope. Some of the men in front had already encountered the enemy, swords flailing. Bodies fell like flies, limbs hit the ground with a huge thud. Salim apparently, to the surprise of those around him, built up some courage, a burst of energy, maybe even of patriotism, he ran forwards, faster than any of the other foot soldiers, perhaps even as fast as a horse. Sayid saw Salim swoop at a soldier in bright red armour, the colour of the enemy. Red liquid dripped from point of Salim's sword. Suddenly, a strike to Salim's head, and he fell, limp and wilted to the ground. Salim's body returned to the earth for good. A scene played out within Sayid's mind, a young general would knock solemnly at Salim's home, an old woman would answer, and the general would give the news of the tragic loss. Her eldest son was dead, lost to what would then be called a war of peace. The old woman would hold her composure until the general excused himself, then her tears would endlessly flow. Her sorrow would be felt for an eternity.

Right and left, front and back, Sayid could see the soldiers falling, falling from both sides. Friend and enemy joined in death, falling together. Sayid edged ever closer to the frontline of his enemy, gaining pace as he moved. He thought that if only he could reach the enemy trenches, the war would somehow be put to an end. He travelled ever forwards. Just short of the low barbed wire fences in front of his enemy's trenches, he came face to face with an adversary. The bright red of his armour pained Sayid's eyes. They stared into each other, studying each and every line of the others face. It was uncanny how similar they looked beneath the guards that covered them from head to toe. For a moment, Sayid felt a pang of sympathy for the poor young boy stood in front of him, and he almost thought it was reflected in the other boy's eyes, but before he could recall the situation in which he had been placed, he felt the sharp pain of a blade planted in his stomach. He gazed down as the blood poured from his open wound, gasping at the pain. Sayid cried out in agony as he dropped slowly to the ground, almost as if it were in slow motion. He lay silently on his side as blood trickled down his chin to the crushed, muddy, blood filled ground below him. He looked up and saw two red grey clouds part above his head, revealing a beautiful blue sky as the life drained from his defeated eyes.

THE FATE OF THE PROTESTER

Emily Martin (age 17)

Michael Thorne could spend all summer listening to the sounds of The Doors and The Stones through the tinny speakers, the basslines reverberating under his feet and through his body. Every so often, a chant would rise above Mick Jagger or Jim Morrison, the voices of the protesters coming together as one to call for peace in Southeast Asia. The steps of City Hall were hidden under a tier of multicolored shirts and placards made with cheap cardboard and felt-tip pens. Although their numbers may have appeared intimidating – Michael had counted the majority of his graduating class over the past three hours, and it was only 6pm – the people were peaceful, made all the more mellow by the marijuana passed from one to the next with startling ease, a toxic layer of intermittent smoke clouding the landscape.

It was Michael's fourth such rally in as many days, and he knew from previous experiences that once the police came along or it grew dark, they would take their music and their joints and their beer to the beach, where a fire would roar and he would be dragged back to consciousness when the sun peeked over the horizon to find himself under a blanket with a girl whose name he couldn't remember (or hadn't been told to begin with). The plan was to go home, sleep off the unavoidable headache, and then do it all over again that afternoon.

War wouldn't stop itself.

To many, the three-story house with its white picket fence and neatly manicured lawn was the epitome of the American dream. It was terrifyingly stereotypical and picturesque, sitting primly on a street of identical buildings that could never be personal enough to call 'home'. All the mailboxes were painted the same color – Desert Sienna – and the flowerboxes looked like clones of each other. Although there was no regulation stating it had to be so, it was an unspoken rule among the inhabitants of Wrenwood Avenue that things would stay as they were.

Then the war rolled around and changed everything.

Michael often wondered what the neighbors would think if they knew what happened behind closed doors. Sometimes the thunder of his parents' arguments would crash and bang as he lay in bed; once, he'd woken to find a fist-shaped hole in the plaster of one of the walls near the staircase. He hadn't said a word at breakfast, afraid to do or say anything to shatter the illusion of peace. He'd left for school and the hole wasn't there when he'd returned. He doubted the Stanleys next door were aware of the fights that took place once twilight fell; his parents didn't need the cover of darkness anymore, couldn't wait for it. The shroud of waning light was enough.

Luckily, it was a good ten hours or so until dusk, and his shadow was a mere infant as it trotted obediently by his side. His cheap sunglasses plotted against him and sharp rays filtered through, burning his eyes and causing the tribal drummers in his head to pick up the rhythm, never relenting. The walls of white in all directions were too bright and he almost wished for night to arrive early so he could gain a reprieve, but then he sorted through the murky haze of a few too many beers and a joint or two and remembered what happened in the evenings, and the thought quickly sobered him.

The long driveway felt like a walk of shame. He knew the routine: a couple of dozen occasions was more than enough rehearsal time. He had to command his feet to put one in front of the other. Hell, he was too tired and too hungover to tolerate any bullshit he might receive on the other side of that eggshell-white door (a satisfactory choice made by Wrenwood Avenue – not too gloomy but not too attention-seeking, either).

As soon as the door closed, John Thorne, ex-General, boomed, "Where have you been?"

"Out," Michael replied irritably, pushing his way around his father, heading for the stairs.

"Out? At one of your protest rallies?" He could practically taste the bitter tang of the ever-present sneer.

"I'm tired. I just want to sleep. Can we talk about this later?"

John said, "You've left school. We need to discuss your options."

"I told you a thousand times, I want – "

"To be a writer, I know. Face reality: you can't always get what you want." Michael felt the flush creep up his neck. His weariness only added to his irritability, and there was nobody who could burrow under his skin like his father. Towering over him on the fifth step, he bristled and shouted, "If I'm 'facing reality', as you put it, I should face up to the fact that you want me out of here! You only talk to me in order to see the back of me!"

"Enough!" John roared loudly; the clock nearby was scared to tick-tock in case it offended him. "I don't like that attitude, boy. A period of time in a boot camp might change your mind. I know people who could put you there faster than you could curse me over it."

"Boot camp?" Michael echoed in disbelief. "You can't make me fight in that war! It goes against all my beliefs and –"

"You're not old enough to understand."

"But I'm old enough to die?" he asked incredulously.

The vein in his father's forehead throbbed warningly. "Go to bed," John said finally, "and sleep, smoke your cigarettes. But we will discuss this later and you will like it."

Michael opened his mouth to protest but a door opened upstairs and his mother's form appeared over the railing, a half-empty bottle of vodka clutched tightly in one fist. "What's going on?"

Father and son stared at each other for a long moment before Michael sighed, ran a hand through his shaggy hair, and said, "Nothing."

He was lying on the thinnest mattress in the world, and he wasn't a man prone to hyperbole. Sleeping on the cold floor may have been preferable – at least then there wouldn't be a spring sticking up his ass.

The dormitory-style room took some getting used to and Michael suspected he needed more time. He had never been a heavy sleeper at home but a natural instinct of self-preservation kicked in when he was suddenly surrounded by scores of men – boys – from all walks of life. Some found it funny to pour water over others while they were deep in unsuspecting dreams; Platt, a few mattresses down on the left, had come in from a training exercise one day to find a dead rat underneath the sheet. There had been raucous laughter but he had only picked it up by the limp tail and carried it outside before stretching out over the skeletal excuse of a bed. He hadn't said a word. Still, Michael had noticed a couple of fellow recruits inspecting their already-stained mattresses for new unwelcome additions before settling.

The first few days had been the toughest, when the night air was permeated with the grunts and snores of strangers. Each rustling of the sheets, like crunchy fall leaves, had him jolting awake with the unfamiliarity of it all. Soon, the physical activity began to take its toll, and sleep came easier. Some days he ran until his muscles screamed 'uncle!' and he collapsed onto the under-stuffed slab, his exhausted body recuperating in less-than-ideal conditions. He pulled his weight so he was left alone, for the most part, and he could rest easier at night.

He was aware of the tips of his toes sticking out from the bottom of the standard-issue blanket, and he could smell a stale fart (probably one of Hill's; he really knew how to let one rip), but he was still dozing and his thoughts and dreams mingled into an impossible reality. In some far-off, dusty alcove of his conscious, he heard a loud bang, some muffled shouting, and then the sheet was ripped from his body by an angry hand. "Thorne!"

Michael shot to his feet too fast, tripping over his own limbs as the blood rushed to his head, and stood shivering in a thin t-shirt and boxer shorts, saluting with a quivering arm.

"Are you deaf, Private?"

"Sir! No, sir!"

"Nice of you to finally join your fellow recruits. You kept these men waiting forty-six seconds, you lazy f-----r, and now your platoon have been assigned forty-six push-ups, one for each second it took you to get your idle ass out of bed."

The recruits grumbled but lowered themselves to the ground all the same. "You're going to pay for this, Thorne," a muscular blond with a skull and crossbones tattoo muttered.

Welcome to the Army.

★ ★ ★

Michael stepped off the helicopter amid a whirlwind of Vietnamese dust, the jungle less than half a football field away virtually obscured, and what was visible was masked in a haze of dry soil. The humidity pressed on his chest and lungs, heavier even than his pack, and dankness enveloped everything with a greedy, clenched fist. Stood in the shelter of the chopper's rotors, he could see uniformed men shouting and pointing, their mouths moving but the sound too weak to reach his ears. It was almost comical, like one of the Charlie Chaplin silent movies he enjoyed watching, except there was no laughter either.

He wondered if this place was actually Hell in pitiful disguise.

Jostled away from the helicopter by a myriad of other recruits, he stumbled to the tree line and watched with old eyes as the blades made their rotations, soon so fast as to be nothing more than an indistinguishable blur, and it took off without regrets. Michael was tempted to chase after it, to catch it and beg the pilot to take him back home to his proud parents and forlorn girlfriend, grieving like a widow at his departure to a foreign land where so many had lost their lives. But he stayed where he was despite every natural instinct screaming at him to move. He was a soldier now, and soldiers didn't make their own orders: they followed them, sheep in khaki camouflage, just another number obeying to the letter.

Surrounded by a sea of green (a color he would quickly learn to hate), occasionally marked with one pale face or another, he barely noticed a platoon jog past on a practice drill. He definitely missed the smirks and nudges as they placed bets on which of the newbies would survive the longest. Nobody picked him.

The ground quaked underfoot and he stumbled in surprise, eyes wide at the sudden and violent change in terrain. He managed to compose himself before anyone saw. Fright did not exist, his commanding officer had repeatedly stated, it is only a state of mind. And, to his horror, Michael had started to believe him. There was something about the authoritarian tone which made it hard to resist; as much as he tried, the propaganda was a python tightening around his neck, and despite it being so stiflingly difficult to breathe, he knew the relief would come when the defense mechanisms kicked in and he would pass out, becoming unaware of the pain inflicted upon his weak body. Someday soon, he was certain he would forget all he had marched for and become indoctrinated to a set of beliefs he didn't subscribe to.

A crowd had gathered outside City Hall. From a distance, he could see the swarm of protestors, could hear the raised voices above the general murmurings. He started to walk closer, his heavy boots and military-issue pack making an all-out run fool-hardy in such intense heat and humidity. No placards this time, no homemade signs of complaint. He could smell smoke, though, and broke into a trot, encouraged by the familiar scent.

He grew closer, closer still, close enough to recognize his friends and companions. He called out to them with glee, waving, smiling. A thousand eyes turned on him as he slowed before the crowd.

"Traitor."

"Hypocrite."

"Coward."

Insults rang like the bells of Notre Dame, loud and clear, and he felt his heart race in his chest. This was wrong. This was all wrong. It wasn't supposed to be like this. He'd grown up with these people, had marched alongside them for justice, and now they were turning on him! Someone spat on his khaki uniform. He backed away slowly, preparing to run, spinning on his heels with his back to the mob.

"Michael!"

He stopped, faced them, recoiled in horror. Vietnamese children, missing limbs and organs, looked back at him with accusatory eyes. The stench of smoke once again was strong but this time he knew it wasn't cigarettes or drugs; he'd been surrounded by the pervasive odor enough to know it was burning flesh. He gagged once, twice, made himself to pay attention to the bodies lining the steps of City Hall. Nobody spoke. Nobody moved. They just stared at him with blank expressions, forcing him to acknowledge what he had done.

Suddenly, and in a move so synchronized he thought it

must have been rehearsed, they all looked to the skies expect-
antly. Michael followed their gaze. He noticed when the planes
came into view, when they dropped their load, when the bombs
streaked through the air and careened towards the earth below,
right on target to –

He woke up in a cold sweat.

Rome may have burned for almost a week but the small village
near Dong Hoi wouldn't survive that long. The stilted huts lining
the beach might have been able to withstand the pounding of the
tides but napalm was out of its league. He'd watched the choppers
fly over, their threatening messages and crude dedications clear to
all in the mid-morning light, and had witnessed the bombs being
dropped from a distance. He'd known the exact moment they had
hit. The fire had roared up from the jungle floor, a beast awakened,
and the smoke billowed after. That was how it was in Vietnam:
nothing followed the rules.

He almost hoped it would rain – at least then somebody would
be crying for the dead and the wounded. Screams of the injured
carried on the wind like perverse birdsong; the quick blasts of
gunfire from the attacking platoons soon silenced the foreign
pleas and he was back to listening to the insects, his own steady
breathing, and the rustle of leaves indicative of an approaching
Charlie. He hadn't moved in four hours.

The stagnant water encased his lower body, forcing his uniform
to stick to his skin in a desperate act of self-preservation. It was
hot and it was humid and it stank to high heaven, and yet he
maintained his position because he hadn't been given new orders.
To move out of turn in enemy territory was suicide. You didn't
eat. You didn't drink. If you wanted to piss, you did it right there
and then. And if you weren't shot, blown up, or captured during
your patrol, you trudged back to camp and waited to do it all over
again in a few more hours.

His eyes flickered from the flames in the distance to the leech
that had started to assault his forearm before the chopper attack.
It was a fat little bugger, full to bursting due to its vampirism.
Survival of the fittest, he mused, only doing what it needs to do to

keep on breathing. Just like he told himself he was doing when he woke in a cold sweat every night with the screams of a thousand Vietnamese innocents ringing in his ears.

Giving his surroundings a quick sweep, confident he was alone, he plucked the offending parasite from his skin and tossed it carelessly into the foliage on his right. Staring at the wound left behind in its wake, he felt no pain. Warfare had rendered him emotionless; he had long since become desensitized to the violence people inflicted upon each other. In the Government's eyes, he was the perfect soldier, an ideal killing machine who obeyed orders without question or judgment, and who felt no qualms at what he had become. He had changed, he knew, and he was slowly losing his grip on his old self. Day by day, his self-knowledge grew weaker and a robot took his place. If he wasn't careful, he could lose his mind.

He wondered if it was still his to give away.

Aden Christmas

David Nicholls

December. Aden 1965. An aggressively hot and dusty place surrounded by harsh grey mountains and arid tracts of sandy desert. A place too, where the hatred of the local populace for us British servicemen was a palpable force daily translated into acts of murder and terrorism. An environment where death lurked in an empty beer can by the roadside, a provocative poster wired to a roadside bomb or in many everyday objects booby trapped to maim and kill. Where sudden sniper fire and grenade attack were expected at any time. A situation where it was essential to venture forth only in groups of at least three, warily suspicious, armed and prepared to open fire to defend yourself.

Not then a good place for celebration of the season of goodwill for the Army, Royal Air Force or Royal Navy personnel stationed far from home and the company of loved ones at this time of year. There were no mobile phones for a quick call home then, no webcams, no email and computers as we use them now were a science fiction dream.

Links with home then were a matter of sitting down quietly and applying pen to paper while trying to keep the sweat in that ferocious heat from dripping onto the page. Telephone calls home were available but expensive and uncertain so letter writing was the main means of keeping in touch with wife and family.

However, we were there and had to make the best of it. 'If you can't take a joke you shouldn't have joined' was the usual wry comment when anyone complained.

As Christmas Day approached celebrations were organised. Parties in the mostly male dominated service establishments, in which alcohol was the mainspring of the merriment or the means of temporarily forgetting the separation from family and friends at home. The Forces Radio service broadcast special request programmes from relatives in Britain, Christmas decorations went up as we all tried to make our lives festive for a few days.

It was the Christmas Carol Service that made that Aden 1965

so memorable for me. The Padres who looked after our spiritual welfare and did so much to 'ease our troubled minds' in other more practical ways, arranged an inter-denominational Carol Service in the open air on a clear space in the centre of Royal Air Force Station Steamer Point.

Hundreds of us made our way down to the place on a night exactly like the night of the Nativity as legend would have us believe. A deep purple unclouded sky with larger-than-life brilliant stars in the clear atmosphere. No Angel of the Lord on High but just the jarring note of a helicopter, its blades whop-whopping away to remind us that someone up there had to keep an eye open for the terrorists.

As the old familiar carols ascended into the night sky many a lump was brought into the throat of us lonely soldiers, sailors and airmen in that hostile country. Afterwards as we streamed away to our barracks we felt something of the spirit of Christmas and somehow nearer to our loved ones so far away.

Yes, I shall always remember my Aden Christmas.

Ted And Ed

Ian Lavan

So at last it was over, the war in Europe. Europe was finally free and Ted, as he had done for the last four years, adjusted his cracked tatty cap, then after checking the pockets of his leather jerkin he shook the worn smooth reins as a signal for Ed to start pulling the cart. It was a daily chore for them both, but somehow after all the years the smell of horse and man comforted each other in the morning. Ed as usual pulled to the right a combination of the loss of one eye and a deep shrapnel scar on his right shoulder.

"Come on lad," Ted steadied Ed as he had many times before and they set off down the track, following the wheel ruts that partitioned the grass.

As they approached the lane the sound of a far distant engine spooked them both, Ted quickly got down from the comfortingly creaking cart to reassure old Ed.

"No bombs, lad, no more bombs," Ted soothed, while stroking the white flash on Ed's nose.

Ed in turn, responded by snuffling an understanding into that ticklish place between Ted's greying mouton-chops and neck, and then set about systematically searching, playing the game for the wizened sweet windfall apple that Ted always kept somewhere. Both were very tired, but now knowing that the war was over and this was to be their last journey, eased aching joints.

"Come on lazy bones," Ted laughed and Ed responded with a steady hypnotic clip-clop, clip-clop, slow enough for Ted to easily limp beside him. Ted's mind wandered for a minute, back to all the journeys they had made, never complaining always doing what they had had to do, two friends now on their last mission, their last journey, finally they would get to rest from what Ted had told Ed was their 'drudge trudge'.

Ted stumbled breaking his reverie and Ed stopped to stretch out his neck to steady him. Clinging tightly to the old horse, Ted slowly came back to were he was and what he was doing, Ed waited patently for him to regain his balance.

"Glad we are together at the end old feller," with this a tear rolled down Ted's cheek, the weary horse gently wiped it onto his muzzle then gave him a firm but tender shut-up-you-old-codger nudge on the arm with his nose.

"Okay, okay," Ted responded with a smile as they set off again, Ed taking most of Ted's weight. "Do you know, Ed, this is my favourite time of the year, just look at the flowers in the hedges, they smell fresh and new." Ed nodded knowingly with a snort. "Everything's clean, bright and light, not old and dirty from war and the dust of men. It's a good time for it all to be over Ed, it's a good time for it to be over."

They clip-clopped on stopping briefly at the crossroads, somehow Ted knew Ed knew what was going on as they didn't turn right as they normally did, they moved straight on trusting each other as they had done from the day they met. Intuitively both of them understood what was going to finally happen.

"At last it's over Ed, we're finally free," Ted explained as they approach the sign.

They stopped for a while in the dappled sunlight as Ted had something to do.

Ed made off as if to go and eat grass, yet never took a mouthful as he kept watch and guard ensuring nothing disturbed them. Ted with one leg stretch out in front while the other bent at the knee and creaked him slowly to the floor then set about scratching the sign with a small knife. Ted stopped, his torso trembling with years of pain and hurt, as the tears came he dropped the knife on the road and bowed his head.

Ed just waited watching until Ted eased himself and sat back up. Then as he came to snuffle Ted he nudged the knife back to him and stood head bowed as if he was reading the sign.

Ted his spirits now lifted, finished what he had to do. "What do you think lad?"

Ed nodded, and then bent to help Ted back to his feet. With what was their last look at the sign, both of them set off again.

Finally they felt the full relief that it truly was all over, no more war, evermore, as they clip-clopped on, friends forever.

The sign is still there on the outskirts of the village. Its now faded writing says,

> *Never forgotten, here lay the bodies of Ted and Ed,*
> *even one of Hitler's bombs could not separate them.*

And underneath roughly carved into the wood, worn and aged is written,

Now Resting – In – Peace.

WHEN HMS ALAMEIN MET THE ARGYLS IN CYPRUS

Ken Stephenson

It was during 'the troubles' that *HMS Alamein* was sent to patrol the waters around Cyprus. British Servicemen were considered legitimate targets for the Eoka gunmen so ordinary shore leave was not an option. Any shore leave was limited to sports events within British Army bases, so the Naval Senior Rates challenged the Army Warrant Officers of the Argyle and Southerland Light Infantry to a football match.

ARMY v NAVY ~ ENGLAND v SCOTLAND.

It promised to be a memorable match – and it was. The teams lined up, the Regimental Sergeant Major appointed himself as the referee and he appointed two sergeants as linesmen. Soon after the start Alamein swept down the field and scored great goal. The RSM pointed to a spot well away from goal and declared 'offside'. The Chief who had scored the goal protested that there had been three defenders on the goal line. The RSM gave three blasts on his whistle. At this signal there appeared beside the protesting Chief, two enormous 'Redcaps' and the Chief was hauled off to the Guardroom.

Shortly after this, the Argyles went on the attack and took a shot at goal, the PO playing at full back cleared off the line. The RSM pointed to the spot 'Penalty kick, dangerous kicking'. The PO objected, that the ball was only a foot off the ground and there wasn't another player near him. The RSM blew his whistle three times and the luckless PO went to the Guardroom between the two enormous Redcaps.

The Argyles missed the penalty.

By half time the Navy team was reduced to a goalkeeper plus six, and the score was 0–0. By three quarter time, the Navy was down to a goalkeeper and one player and the score was 1–0 to the Navy and this was the final score.

The Argyles demanded revenge for this defeat and so another sports leave was arranged. The RSM refereed the match again and the result was a goalless draw. This was not really surprising, we only played one minute each way. I'm not to sure what happened later, but I think the Argyles won the 'mess games', most games involving lots of whisky with the RSM acting as referee.

We had quite a few more sports leaves to play football but we never saw another goal. It is difficult to score in one minute, especially one minute on the RSM's watch.

Before we left Cyprus we had an onboard day for the Argyles. Now *HMS Alamein* had an excellent Water Polo team. We had taken on all comers in the Med and had defeated them all. So we challenged the Argyles to a Water Polo Match and they duly accepted.

Water Polo at sea is played with the goals suspended from two booms projecting from the ship side; this means there is no bottom. The Alamein team entered the water – they looked formidable, every one in the team floating with top half of his torso well above the water line. Then the Argyle team appeared on the upper deck, they looked too small, too thin and really they did not look like a Water Polo team Our First Lieutenant appeared just in time to hear the Sergeant ordering a young soldier into the water.

"But I can't swim, Sergeant."

The Sergeant was unmoved. "I said get in the water."

"But Sergeant…"

The First Lieutenant intervened: "Sergeant, if the man cannot swim then he cannot go in the water."

The Sergeant was adamant. "He will go in the water, sir. There are three of our soldiers who cannot swim. I myself cannot swim but we are all going in. We have been challenged and we, the Argyles, have never ever refused a challenge… and we have to accept the challenge."

The First Lieutenant. was in a quandary and asked the Sergeant what could be done to stop the match.

The solution was simple: Alamein must concede the match

We conceded. That was the only water polo match that *HMS Alamein* ever lost, and we lost it to a team with four soldiers who could not swim.

Of course human nature ensures that we only remember these

good times, although at least once a year, we do try to remember the friends that we lost when things did go wrong.

HMS *Alamein* lost three sailors during our spell in Cyprus; we never knew how many soldiers the Argyles lost

Voices of the Poppies – An Anthology of Poetry
(Introduced by Dame Vera Lynn DBE)
ISBN 9781906236076
£8.99
(Proceeds to FLOW for All)

Poems of the Poppies – An Anthology of Poetry Volume 1
ISBN 9781906236250
£8.99
(Proceeds to FLOW for All)

A Tapestry of Verse
by Dennis Shrubshall
ISBN 9781906236144
£8.99
(proceeds shared between The British Limbless ex Servicemen's Association, Combat Stress, and The National Gulf Veterans and Families Association)

Overpaid, Over-Sexed and Over There
(The Adventures of a Limey in the US Army)
by Chris Holloway
ISBN 9781906236168
£8.99

Surviving Changi – A Memoir
(With illustrations by kind courtesy of Ronald Searle)
by Peter Gordon Kendall
ISBN 9781906236014
£14.00

Lightning Source UK Ltd.
Milton Keynes UK
15 November 2009